Was Caitlyn up to the responsibility she'd inherited?

Steve studied her, frownin[illegible] [illegible]bered her well, even th[illegible] [illegible]hind him in school. [illegible] of the fierce ambit[illegible]

She'd used that s[illegible] [illegible]ion of hers to take the big cit[illegible] [illegible] what he could see, apparently she'd n[illegible], despite all the obstacles there must have been for a girl from Texas with no money.

And now, Caitlyn Villard had grown into a beauty—if you liked women who were sophisticated, even icy. But the important thing wasn't how she looked. What was crucial was whether she could be a mother to her twin nieces.

* * *

Homecoming Heroes: Saving children and finding love deep in the heart of Texas

Mission: Motherhood—Marta Perry (LI#452)
July 2008
Lone Star Secret—Lenora Worth (LI#456)
August 2008
At His Command—Brenda Coulter (LI#460)
September 2008
A Matter of the Heart—Patricia Davids (LI#464)
October 2008
A Texas Thanksgiving—Margaret Daley (LI#468)
November 2008
Homefront Holiday—Jillian Hart (LI#472)
December 2008

Books by Marta Perry

Love Inspired

A Father's Promise #41
Since You've Been Gone #75
**Desperately Seeking Dad* #91
**The Doctor Next Door* #104
**Father Most Blessed* #128
A Father's Place #153
***Hunter's Bride* #172
***A Mother's Wish* #185
***A Time To Forgive* #193
***Promise Forever* #209
Always in Her Heart #220
The Doctor's Christmas #232
True Devotion #241
†*Hero in Her Heart* #249
†*Unlikely Hero* #287
†*Hero Dad* #296
†*Her Only Hero* #313
†*Hearts Afire* #380
†*Restless Hearts* #388
†*A Soldier's Heart* #396
Mission: Motherhood #452

*Hometown Heroes
**Caldwell Kin
†The Flanagans

Love Inspired Suspense

In the Enemy's Sights #20
Land's End #24
Tangled Memories #28
Season of Secrets #32
‡*Hide in Plain Sight* #65
‡*A Christmas to Die For* #75
‡*Buried Sins* #80
Final Justice #104

‡The Three Sisters Inn

MARTA PERRY

has written everything from Sunday school curriculum to travel articles to magazine stories in more than twenty years of writing, but she feels she's found her writing home in the stories she writes for Love Inspired.

Marta lives in rural Pennsylvania, but she and her husband spend part of each year at their second home in South Carolina. When she's not writing, she's probably visiting her children and her six beautiful grandchildren, traveling, gardening or relaxing with a good book.

Marta loves hearing from readers, and she'll write back with a signed bookmark or her brochure of Pennsylvania Dutch recipes. Write to her c/o Steeple Hill Books, 233 Broadway, Suite 1001, New York, NY 10279, e-mail her at marta@martaperry.com, or visit her on the Web at www.martaperry.com.

Mission: Motherhood

Marta Perry

Published by Steeple Hill Books™

Special thanks and acknowledgment to Marta Perry for her contribution to the Homecoming Heroes miniseries

STEEPLE HILL BOOKS

ISBN-13: 978-0-373-87488-0
ISBN-10: 0-373-87488-X

MISSION: MOTHERHOOD

This edition published by arrangement with Steeple Hill Books.

www.SteepleHill.com

Printed in U.S.A.

Bear one another's burdens,
and so fulfill the law of Christ.
—*Galatians* 6:2

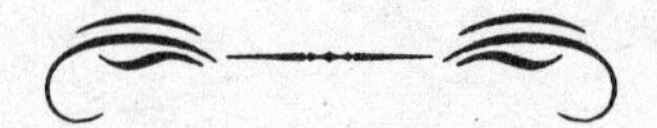

This story is dedicated to the Love Inspired sisters
who worked on this continuity series—
Lenora, Brenda, Pat, Margaret and Jillian.
And, as always, to Brian, with much love.

Chapter One

It had taken ten years in New York City to eliminate all traces of Texas from Caitlyn Villard's voice. It took only a week in Prairie Springs to bring it back again.

Had she really just said *y'all* to the kindergarten teacher and her own twin nieces? Caitlyn stepped out into the courtyard of the Prairie Springs Elementary School. She was greeted by a blast of air hot enough to wilt her hairstyle and melt the makeup from her face.

"Um, ma'am?" The warm drawl came from above.

She looked up. A lanky man clung to the top of a wooden stepladder, a paint can in one hand and a dripping brush in the other. "You might want to move out of range a bit."

"Sorry." She took a few steps away, standing under the shade of the roof overhang. She had obviously forgotten just how hot Texas was in July.

Through the window she could see into the room where Amanda and Josie sat at a round table with Sarah Alpert, who was assessing their readiness to start kindergarten in September.

That was still two months away. By the time the twins started school, she would be back in New York, picking up the threads of her interrupted life. Back on the fast track to partner at Graham, Graham and Welch, one of the Big Apple's most prestigious law firms. This interval in Texas, helping her mother cope with the aftermath of her sister's death, would be a memory.

"You brought the girls in for their first taste of kindergarten, did you?"

Caitlyn blinked, as startled as if the spindly potted shrub next to the door had made a personal remark. The painter had descended—tall, lanky, wearing the scuffed boots, blue jeans, western belt and ball cap that were almost a uniform here.

"I beg your pardon?" It was a tone designed to freeze unwelcome attention.

"The twins," he said, as if she was a bit slow on the uptake. "I bet they're excited about starting kindergarten in the fall."

His eyes, intensely blue in a lean, tanned face, now held amusement. They also seemed vaguely familiar.

"I'm sorry. Do I know you?"

"Well, now, I reckon I'm just not as memorable as I thought I was." He didn't look as if he believed that, in spite of the aw-shucks expression he wore. He tipped the ball cap politely. "Steve Windham. Prairie Springs High School. Ring any bells?"

She had to dredge through memories she'd happily buried a long time ago. "Steve Windham. I guess so. You were a senior when I was a freshman, I think."

Actually she knew, but she didn't intend to pander to the man's self-conceit. He looked far too pleased with himself already.

She let her gaze wander over what had to be at least six feet or more of solid muscle. Steve had been the star athlete of his class, and he still looked it. He'd been the valedictorian, too, and probably voted most likely to succeed.

"That'd be about right," he agreed. "That was way too many years ago, I guess."

"And after high school you became a housepainter, did you? I thought I remembered that you had an athletic scholarship to one of the big schools."

That was typical of Prairie Springs. People just settled down to live the way their folks had, instead of getting out into the world and making a mark. Being a painter was fine, if that was what you really wanted, but it was hard to believe someone with Steve's intelligence and talent hadn't had any bigger goals.

Steve's right eyebrow cocked, giving him a quizzical look. "I don't guess there's anything wrong with painting. It's an honest day's work. So what did Ms. Caitlyn Villard turn out to be?"

She hadn't meant to insult the man, and realized maybe she had been a little judgmental. It wasn't any of her business how Steve Windham spent his life.

"I'm an attorney in New York."

That eyebrow lifted a little higher. "Only now you're back in Prairie Springs. Going to practice law here, are you?"

She hoped the horror she felt at his suggestion didn't show on her face.

She managed what she hoped was a polite smile. "You'll have to excuse me. I think the teacher is ready for me to come back in."

He nodded, still with that faintly amused grin on his lips.

She hurried away, aware that he stood there staring after her, with his thumbs hooked nonchalantly in his belt.

Get out of Prairie Springs. That had been her only goal back in high school.

Well, now she'd come full circle. Getting out of Prairie Springs was her only goal now.

Sarah Alpert, the kindergarten teacher, gave Caitlyn a welcoming smile as she reentered the classroom. A slim, fine-boned redhead, she seemed to exude warmth, and her casual jeans and shirt made the situation feel less formal for her young prospective students.

She rose from her place at the low table where she'd been sitting with the twins.

"You girls can finish up your pictures while I talk with your aunt, all right?"

Amanda, the older by twenty minutes, looked a little rebellious at the prospect of sitting still, but she turned back to her picture at Ms. Alpert's firm gaze. Josie never lifted her eyes from the page, appearing lost in whatever she was drawing.

The twins were physically identical, with their straight, chestnut-colored hair and big blue eyes, but they were very different in personality. Caitlyn got them right about eighty percent of the time, and probably the teacher, with her experience, would quickly figure out how to tell them apart.

Sarah led the way to her desk at the end of the room, where they'd have a little privacy. She nodded to a folding chair she'd put at right angles to the desk, and Caitlyn sat down.

"How did they do?"

Caitlyn was surprised to find that she had any apprehension about it. She'd only seen the twins a handful of times in their young lives, but they seemed bright. Certainly her younger sister, Carolyn, had been intelligent, even if she'd scorned the education Caitlyn had always thirsted for.

"They're certainly ready intellectually for kindergarten."

"That's good." That was why they were here, after all, wasn't it?

But the teacher's gaze still expressed some concern. "As to how they'll be dealing with their loss in another two months, I just don't know. I guess we'll see where they are then. Grief from the loss of both parents could affect their adjustment."

"I hadn't thought of that." There were, it appeared, a lot of things she hadn't thought of. Well, what did she know about five-year-olds?

Sarah Alpert nodded sympathetically. "Have you noticed many changes in them since they learned that their parents were gone?"

"I haven't—I mean, my job in New York keeps me very busy. My mother was taking care of the twins after my sister and her husband were deployed."

"Yes, of course. I know that. You have my sympathy for your loss."

"Thank you." Her throat tightened on the words.

Carolyn and Dean, her husband, both gone in an instant on the other side of the world. That was something people in Prairie Springs must have to get used to, living as they did in the shadow of the army's Fort Bonnell.

She cleared her throat. "In any event, my mother says that Amanda has been more mischievous than usual, and

Josie more withdrawn, although she's always been the shyer of the two. Ms. Alpert—"

"Call me Sarah, please." The teacher reached across the desk to press her hand. "We all know each other here, and your mother and I have often worked on church suppers together."

"Yes, she said that she knew you. She wanted me to mention to you that Josie will follow wherever Amanda leads, even if it's into trouble."

Sarah smiled. "I'll keep that in mind. I know your mother is very relieved to have you here to take over with the children. You are staying, aren't you?"

Did everyone think that? She supposed she owed the teacher an answer, even if she didn't owe one to Steve Windham.

"I'm not sure how long I'll be here. My career is in New York." That sounded sufficiently vague, when the truth was that she longed to get back to her own life, even though duty demanded that she be here for the moment, at least.

"You might find something to do here in Prairie Springs," Sarah suggested. "I know it isn't really my business to interfere, but I'm concerned about the children. They've been through a rough time, and it would be a shame to uproot them at this point."

It was impossible to take offense at Sarah's comments, given the warmth and concern that shimmered in her blue eyes. And she'd brought up a good point—one that Caitlyn hadn't really considered. Caitlyn's original plan had been to take a month's leave, help her mother and the children recover from their grief and see them settled financially, and then get back to her own life.

That plan had seemed reasonable back in New York, when she was scrambling to get time off work, turn her cases over to someone else and get here in time for the funerals. Now that she was on the spot, things weren't so clear-cut.

"I can't practice law here. I'm not licensed in Texas, and I haven't even considered that. I have to admit, though, that it wouldn't be a bad idea for me to find something part-time to do while I'm here."

She hadn't imagined finances would be an issue when she'd taken a leave of absence, but then, she'd never tried to do without her salary before. She hoped she'd be able to continue working on some cases from here, but it had been made clear to her that the clients of Graham, Graham and Welsh expected and would receive personal attention. At least they were willing to hold her position open.

No one could live on her salary in Manhattan, pay off college and law school loans and still have much left over anyway. When she made partner, it would be another story, but in the meantime, her finances were tight. And her mother had given up her job at the gift shop when Carolyn and Dean were deployed to the Middle East.

The twins had the funds that had come to them on their parents' deaths, of course, but if possible, Mama wanted that put away for their futures.

"You know, I believe I might know just the thing." Sarah looked pleased at the prospect of helping. She turned to her desk and scribbled something on a piece of paper. "I volunteer at Children of the Day. It's a local charity that helps victims of war—does wonderful work. As it happens, they're looking for a care coordinator right now, and I believe the schedule would be flexible. With your legal background, you'd probably be a big asset."

"I'm not licensed in Texas—" she repeated, but Sarah pressed the paper into her hand.

"Just talk to Anna Terenkov, the director. I'm sure this is all going to work out fine."

Sarah was a lot more optimistic than she was, since at the moment she didn't see anything working out fine. Still, if she could get the job, the money would be welcome. Her expenses in New York continued unabated while she kicked her heels in Texas.

Not for long, she reminded herself. She'd do all she could for her mother and the twins, since Carolyn had named her as their guardian, but in the end, her life was back in New York.

Steve worked his way methodically through cleaning up the paintbrushes. He'd volunteered two hours of painting to the elementary school this afternoon, but he had a meeting back on post at four. The group he'd formed to get soldiers to volunteer for community projects was going strong now, and he owed it to the people he'd talked into it to show that he'd be right in there volunteering his own time and effort.

From where he stood, he could see through the windows of the kindergarten room. Amanda and Josie, chestnut heads together, whispered over their papers, while their aunt Caitlyn sat talking with Sarah Alpert.

He worried about the twins, as he worried about all those under his care who had suffered losses. The twins had each other and their grandmother, and now they had their aunt. Was Caitlyn up to the responsibility she'd inherited from her sister?

He studied her, frowning a little. He remembered her well, which was odd in itself since she'd been three years behind him in school. Maybe she'd stood apart because of the fierce ambition she'd shown at an age when most girls were too busy giggling over boys, pop stars and clothes to give much thought to their futures.

Now—well, Caitlyn Villard had grown into a beauty, if you liked women who were sophisticated, even icy. She was tall and slim, carrying herself as if there wasn't a doubt in her mind as to who she was and where she was headed.

The hair that had once been flaxen was now a rich golden brown, tousled in a way that he suspected was style, not nature. Her eyes hadn't changed, though. They were a warm hazel with glints of gold when the sun caught them.

Well, the important thing wasn't how she looked, although she was certainly worth a second glance from any man. What was crucial was whether she could take care of those children.

She'd probably used that single-minded determination of hers that he remembered to take the big city by storm. From what he could see, apparently she'd made it, despite all the obstacles there must have been for a little girl from Texas with no family backing or money.

But now she was faced with even harder barriers in learning how to be a mother to two precious children. Did she have that in her? He didn't know.

His thoughts automatically went inward in prayer. *Lord, You know what You have in mind for Amanda and Josie, and for their aunt. If there's a way in which I can help, please use me.*

When he looked again, the door was opening and Caitlyn and the twins were coming out.

Amanda spotted him first and let out a squeal. She came running toward him, waving a welcome, with Josie scurrying behind.

He bent to hug them, holding them away from his paint stains and grinning at their enthusiastic greeting. "Hey, you two. Y'all been having some fun in the kindergarten room with Miss Sarah?"

"I made a picture and printed my name," Amanda said importantly. "And I said my numbers, too."

"How about you, sugar?" He tugged gently at a strand of Josie's hair. Josie always had to be coaxed a little. "Did you print your name, too?"

She nodded. "I printed Josie," she said. "Not Josephine."

"Girls." Caitlyn had reached them by now, and she clearly didn't know what to make of this. "What are you doing?"

He smiled at her. "The twins and I are old friends." He caught Amanda's hand as she reached for the paint can. "That's wet, Amanda."

Amanda pouted for a fraction of a second before turning to her aunt. "We love Chaplain Steve," she said. "He's our friend."

"*Chaplain* Steve?" Caitlyn's voice accented the title, and annoyance danced in her eyes. "Are you really a minister?"

He shrugged. "Guilty."

"You knew I thought you were a painter." Her lips tightened.

Obviously Caitlyn didn't like being fooled. "Sorry."

Truth to tell, he felt a little embarrassed that he hadn't been up front with her. "I did know what you were thinking, but you looked so disapproving I couldn't resist teasing you just a mite."

Faint color came up on her cheeks. "I wasn't disapproving. It's nothing to me what you do."

"Come on, now," he said. "Tell me you weren't thinking that I'd failed to live up to my potential, like Mrs. Clemente used to say in trigonometry class."

Josie tugged at his sleeve. "What does potential mean?" She said the word carefully.

"It means doing everything that you're able to do," Steve answered.

"Oh." She seemed to be storing the definition away for possible future use.

"As I recall, your father was a chaplain, wasn't he?" Caitlyn had herself in hand now, and she asked the question with just the right degree of polite interest.

"That's right. I guess I could have been assigned most anyplace, but I requested Fort Bonnell, and here I am. I've taken over the Fort Bonnell Christian Chapel, but I had to redecorate, since Daddy took all his fishing pictures with him when he and Mama retired to Wyoming."

"And you know the twins how?" Her voice expressed doubt.

"They're part of my job, as it happens, ministering to those of our Fort Bonnell community who've suffered losses."

He managed to keep his mind from straying to his own loss. "Not that these two adorable ladies aren't more than just a job to me."

"I see." Her face had stiffened at the reminder of

Carolyn and Dean, and he felt a pang of remorse for teasing her as he had. This couldn't be easy for her.

"I'm sorry for your loss. It must be rough."

"Yes." She clipped off the word, as if reluctant to accept sympathy. "Well..." She managed a smile and extended her hand. "It was nice to see you again, Steve."

He took her hand solemnly, a little amused. "Same here. But it's a small town, Caitlyn. I'm sure I'll see you again soon."

Her smile was stiff. "Come on, girls. It's time to go home."

"Don't want to." Amanda pouted, looking dangerously near to stamping her feet. "I want to stay with Chaplain Steve."

"We have to go." Caitlyn held out her hand.

"No." Now Amanda did stamp her foot. "I don't want to."

Josie took a step closer to him, clearly not knowing what to do at this open mutiny, any more than her aunt did. Caitlyn's expression said only too clearly that she wasn't prepared to cope with this.

He knelt next to Amanda, putting one arm reassuringly around Josie. "I'm afraid you can't stay with me, Amanda, because I have to go to a meeting. And I'll bet your grandmother is waiting to hear all about how you did at school, don't you think?"

Amanda pouted a moment longer, as if reluctant to give up her grudge. Then she spun around, holding her picture up. "I'm going to show Grammy my painting. She'll put it on the refrigerator."

"Mine, too," Josie said. "Mine, too."

"She'll put mine up first," Amanda said, and darted toward the car.

"Mine, mine," Josie shrieked, and ran after her sister.

Caitlyn seemed frozen to the spot for another instant. Then she hurried after them without a backward glance for him.

Steve watched them go, frowning a little. Those children were hurting, and he hurt for them. They needed so much. Was Caitlyn going to be able to provide that?

Or had Carolyn Mayhew made the mistake of her life when she named her sister as their guardian?

Chapter Two

Caitlyn knelt beside the bathtub, wondering how two five-year-olds in a tub could so resemble a pondful of frogs.

Amanda bounced up and down on her bottom, sending a wave of soapy water sloshing toward her sister. Josie's squeal echoed from the tile tub surround, and she scrambled backward.

"Easy, Amanda." She caught each twin by a slippery arm. "Don't fall back against the spigot. That would hurt your head."

"I won't." Amanda bounced again. This time the water splashed Caitlyn's sleeve to her shoulder.

"Hey!" Smiling in spite of herself, she splashed Amanda back. "No fair. I'm still dressed, not like you." She tickled a bare dimpled elbow, eliciting a giggle from Amanda.

"I love my bath." That might be the first thing Josie had volunteered since Caitlyn had been here. Usually she waited for a question before speaking, or echoed what her twin had said.

"What do you like about it?" Caitlyn put a plastic doll into a red boat and zoomed it toward her small, shy niece.

Josie managed a hint of a smile. "Giving my dolls 'ventures. They like that."

"Good idea." She let Josie have the boat. "You give your doll an adventure with the boat, while I wash Amanda's hair."

Josie nodded, smiling, but Amanda's face puckered up at the suggestion. What now? Was it ever possible to get both of them happy at the same time?

"I don't want my hair washed." Amanda pouted. "You'll get soap in my eyes."

"No, I won't." Although now that she considered it, she wasn't sure how you managed to shampoo a wiggly child without disaster. "Tell you what. You show me how Grammy does it, and I'll do exactly what you say. You be the director, okay?"

Amanda considered that for a moment, and then she nodded. "But you do 'zactly like I say."

It was a small triumph, but she'd take it. As she shampooed and rinsed, carefully following directions, her thoughts drifted back to the afternoon. Odd, running into Steve Windham like that.

His idea of humor had been more than a little annoying. On the other hand, his concern for the girls had been obvious. And she'd taken note of the way he'd so easily averted Amanda's tantrum by focusing her on the future instead. She'd remember that technique for the next time Amanda rebelled. And there probably would be a next time. Amanda, like her mother, seemed born to test the boundaries.

Maybe Steve had kids of his own. The thought startled her. It was certainly possible, although he hadn't been wearing a wedding ring. And exactly why she'd taken note of that, she wasn't sure.

With one little girl shampooed and one to go, she turned her attention to Josie, who submitted without argument to her shampoo. In a few minutes she was wrapping two wiggling bodies in one large towel.

"Oh my goodness, I've got an armful of eels," she declared, rubbing wet curls. "That's what Grammy used to say when she dried us."

"She says that to us, too," Amanda said. "Now pajamas, and then we'll tell you just what you hafta do to put us to bed."

She nodded, spraying Josie's shoulder-length hair with conditioner before attempting to get a comb through it. This was her first attempt at getting the girls to bed on her own, and she needed all the help she could get.

Finally they were into pajamas and snuggled one on each side of her in their pink-and-white bedroom for a story. She held them close, a little surprised by the strength of affection that swept through her.

If anyone had asked, a few weeks ago, if she loved her nieces, she'd have said yes, but it would have been an abstract emotion. She'd loved them but she hadn't known them. Now all that was changed.

"'The Princess and the Pea,'" she read. "I remember this story. Let's see if it's changed any since I was a little girl."

Amanda giggled. "Stories don't change, Auntie Caitlyn. We read one book and then one Bible story from our *Bible Storybook* that you gave us for Christmas, and then we say prayers."

She opened her mouth to say she hadn't given them a storybook for Christmas, and then shut it again. She'd taken the easy way out and sent a check, and someone, probably Carolyn, had taken the time to buy and wrap presents and put her name on them.

Amanda's innocent assumption made her feel—well, thoughtless, at the least. Surely she could have taken the time to find out what they wanted and buy the gifts on her own.

That faint uneasiness lingered through the stories and prayers. Caitlyn tucked matching pink quilts around them and kissed their rosy cheeks.

"Auntie Caitlyn?" Amanda was frowning. Had she gotten some part of the routine wrong?

"What is it, sweetie?" She smoothed still-damp hair back from Amanda's face.

"Are Mommy and Daddy happy in Heaven?"

Whatever she'd expected, it hadn't been that. A theological question was out of her realm. She wasn't the person to ask. Chaplain Steve, he'd do a better job of this.

"Well, I think so. Have you talked to Grammy about it?"

She nodded. "She says God takes care of them in Heaven, so they must be happy."

"Well, Grammy must know," she said, grateful to have squeaked through that tricky spot.

"But how can they be?" Tears shone in her eyes. "How can they be happy without us?"

She was totally out of her depth now, and her throat was so tight she couldn't have gotten an answer out even if she'd been able to think of one.

Fortunately her mother was there, coming quickly into the room to bend over the bed. She must have been waiting in the hall, giving Caitlyn a chance to finish the bedtime routine.

"Of course they miss you, darling." Mama's voice was

soft. "And that might make them sad sometimes. But they know you're happy and that we're taking care of you, so that makes them happy, too. You see?"

Amanda nodded slowly. Caitlyn suspected the little girl wasn't entirely satisfied, but at least she wasn't asking any other questions that Caitlyn couldn't answer.

Hugs and kisses all around, and then she and her mother were out in the hall, leaving the door open just a crack. "Not too much chatter, now," Mama called as they started down the hall. "You had a big day today."

"Thanks for coming in when you did, Mama." She put her arm around her mother's waist. "I didn't know how to handle that."

Her mother gave her a gentle squeeze. "You'll learn by experience. That's the only way anyone ever learns to be a parent."

Something in her rebelled at that. She wasn't a parent, and she didn't intend to be here long enough to learn. It was on the tip of her tongue to say that, but she closed her lips on the words.

Her mother looked tired, too tired for the sixty-five Caitlyn knew she was. Grief, she supposed, combined with the stress of caring for two lively five-year-olds for the past six months.

"Carolyn and Dean shouldn't have expected you to take over when they were deployed," she said. "It was too much for you."

Mama shrugged. "It's made me realize I'm not as young as I used to be, that's for sure. Taking care of two five-year-olds is a Texas-size job. But you do what you have to do. It's not as if they had any other options."

She wanted to say that they should have been responsible enough not to get in that position to begin with, but her mother wouldn't hear anything critical of Carolyn.

Well, maybe her mother wouldn't admit it, but in Caitlyn's opinion, Carolyn had been too quick to dump her responsibilities on other people.

"Listen, would it be any use if I hired someone to help out a little? With the girls, or the house, or whatever?"

Her mother looked surprised. "That's sweet of you, darling, but I'll be okay now that you're here. The two of us can handle things."

There it was again—that assumption that she was here to stay.

"You're not planning to go away, are you?" Her silence must have lasted too long, and her mother looked so dismayed that she couldn't possibly do anything but deny it.

"Not now, but I have a job possibility at Children of the Day. I'm supposed to go for an interview with the director tomorrow. It's only part-time, but I don't want to burden you—"

"Children of the Day? That's wonderful." Her mother interrupted her with a hug. "You'll love it there. I'm so pleased."

The hug strengthened. Caitlyn hugged her mother back, but the feel of her mother's arms was like fragile, yet strong threads tightening around her, trying to bind her to this place.

"Welcome to Children of the Day. I hope you'll enjoy your work here." Anna Terenkov, the founder and director of the charity, rose from behind her desk after the briefest of interviews, extending her hand.

Caitlyn blinked for a second before she stood to shake the woman's hand. She'd met executives who prided themselves on quick decisions before, but Ms. Terenkov had them beat by a mile.

"Ms. Terenkov—"

"Please, call me Anna." A smile banished her businesslike expression. "We're all on a first-name basis here, volunteers and staff alike."

"Anna." She tried to grasp a situation that seemed to be sliding away from her. "Isn't there anything else you'd like to ask me about my qualifications?"

The director waved that away. "I've seen quite enough to know you'll be an asset to the organization. And, frankly, we're in need of a capable person to step into the care coordinator position. That's one job I don't want to lay on a volunteer, and our last coordinator had to leave quite suddenly."

That sounded ominous. Anna seemed to read her expression and laughed.

"Nothing bad, I assure you. Her husband was transferred to a post in the Northeast, and naturally she and the children went with him."

"He was in the military, I gather."

Anna nodded. "Almost everyone in town has some connection to Fort Bonnell, in one way or another. Now—" she rounded the desk "—let me show you our facility and get you started."

She hadn't imagined being hired that quickly, let alone starting, but she followed the petite blond human dynamo out of her office for a whirlwind tour of the building.

Children of the Day was housed in a gracious slate-blue Victorian on a quiet side street just off Veterans Boulevard,

Prairie Springs's main drag. Sheltered by shrubbery and a white wrought-iron fence, the charming Victorian looked more like an elegant private residence than a nonprofit foundation.

"As you can see, the first floor is dedicated to the organization." Anna waved at the volunteer who was seated behind a desk in the welcoming lobby area. "The kitchen downstairs is for the staff and volunteers, so don't hesitate to use it. My mother and I have our private apartment upstairs."

"Is your mother involved with Children of the Day also?"

Anna smiled. "My mother does a little bit of everything, all with great enthusiasm. You'll see where I get my energy when you meet her. She also runs the grief center at Prairie Springs Christian Church. I think she mentioned that your nieces are involved in her children's program."

Something else Caitlyn hadn't known. She'd have to ask her mother about that. At least the twins were apparently getting some professional help.

Anna led the way to the next room. "This is Laura Dean. Laura, meet Caitlyn Villard, our new care coordinator." Anna paused by a desk in the room behind the lobby.

"It's nice to meet you, Caitlyn." The slim young blonde flashed a welcoming smile. "Especially since I'm sure you're going to take some of the load off my shoulders."

"Laura is officially our secretary, but like everyone else, she does whatever needs to be done. And she does it very well, by the way."

Anna was out of the room before Laura could respond, but Caitlyn guessed Laura was probably used to that.

"This will be your office." Anna ushered her into a high-ceilinged room with windows looking onto a side lawn. It had probably once been a modest parlor, with its small fireplace and beautiful molding, but was now furnished with a computer desk and file cabinets. Several maps were pinned onto a bulletin board on the wall.

Anna waved at the small blue pins that dotted the map. "Those are places where we have programs. We provide food, shelter, medical care, educational programs—anything we can to alleviate the suffering of those touched by war." Anna's passion was impressive.

"It's a big job."

"A huge job," Anna agreed. "Those projects are ongoing, and they're already established and running well. What I need you to do is coordinate the kinds of services we provide for individual special needs that arise frequently."

"I see." She didn't, but surely she was going to get more explanation than that.

Anna bent over the desk for a moment and brought up a file on the computer. "Here's the project I want you to start with. There's very little information yet, but you'll read everything we have."

"Yes, of course."

"Ali Tabiz was orphaned and injured in the fighting. We've been contacted by Dr. Mike Montgomery, a surgeon with the army currently stationed in the Middle East. We've worked with him for a while. Little Ali may need heart surgery, and Mike wants him brought here to see a pediatric cardiac surgeon. That's your job."

So she was supposed to get a minor foreign national out of a war-torn country and bring him to Texas for treatment. She couldn't even begin to ask the questions that flooded her mind.

"Don't panic," Anna said. She pulled out a black three-ring binder. "Our last coordinator was very organized, and we've done this sort of thing many times. She's outlined a step-by-step process with all the things you'll need to do."

Caitlyn grasped the binder as if it were a life preserver and she were sinking under the waves. "Good. I'm going to need it."

"You'll be fine. And I'm just across the hall. Come to me with any questions." She frowned slightly. "Dr. Mike is usually in touch via e-mail, but sometimes things get pretty hot where he is."

"You think that's why you haven't received any other information?" That must mean that the child was in a dangerous place, as well.

"Probably, but we won't waste time. You can start by alerting the medical facilities and personnel we normally use that we'll have a case coming their way. Once we know more, you can get the details nailed down."

Someone tapped on the frame of the open door, and Caitlyn turned to see Sarah, the kindergarten teacher. "Anna, you're needed on the phone. It's some CEO who wants to make a donation and won't talk to anyone else."

"Okay, I'll take it. Never turn down an eager donor." Anna was gone in an instant, leaving Caitlyn with her mouth still open to say goodbye.

She looked at Sarah, who stood there smiling, probably at her expression. "You didn't tell me she was a whirlwind."

Sarah laughed. "How else would she get everything done? Don't worry—you'll get used to it." She waved and disappeared, leaving Caitlyn staring blankly at the computer screen.

She found she was still clutching the binder. All right. She could do this. She needed a job, and here it was. She wouldn't let anything keep her from succeeding at it.

An hour later she was feeling far more confident. As Anna had said, her predecessor had been organized.

She'd already made several calls, and she'd been pleasantly surprised by her reception. The physicians and hospital administrators had obviously worked with Children of the Day in the past and were perfectly ready to jump into the new project. As soon as she had some more information—

That was the sticking point. No one could do anything until they learned a bit more about the case. She checked the e-mail inbox again, feeling a flutter of excitement at a message from Dr. Montgomery. Maybe this was what they needed.

She clicked it open, and a small face appeared on the screen. This, clearly, was Ali Tabiz.

Big brown eyes, short dark brown hair, an engaging smile. According to the brief statistics attached, the little boy was five, the same age as the twins, but he looked—what?

She grappled for the right word. He was small, maybe suffering from the shortages that went along with having a war in your backyard, and there was a bruise over one eye. But he didn't look younger than the twins. In a way, he looked older, as those dark brown eyes seemed to hold a world of sorrows.

"Cute kid." The voice, coming from behind her without warning, startled her so much that her hands jerked from the keys, and she swung around. It was Steve Windham again, this time in uniform. Somehow it made him seem even taller, his shoulders even broader. Or maybe that was because she was sitting down.

She shoved her chair back, standing. "Steve, hello." She noted the bars he wore. "Or should I say Captain Windham?"

He shook his head, giving her that easy smile. "I'm Chaplain Steve to everyone. Since we're old friends, I'm just Steve to you."

She wouldn't, she decided, exactly call them old friends. "First the elementary school, now Children of the Day. Are you following me?"

His grin widened. "Afraid not. Not that that's not a good idea."

Maybe it was safest to ignore the comment. "What are you doing here?"

"I coordinate all the military volunteers who work with Children of the Day, so I'm in and out of the foundation office all the time."

"Painting at the elementary school, volunteering here, counseling the grieving—surely a chaplain's not expected to do all that."

"All that and more." He shrugged. "An army chaplain has a surprising amount of autonomy. His or her duties are what he or she makes of them, outside of regular services. I follow where the Lord leads me to minister, and He led me here."

Which meant she'd be tripping over him, apparently. He'd been right to remind her. Prairie Springs was a small town.

He nodded toward the computer screen. "Is this little guy your first project?"

"Yes."

He lifted an eyebrow. "It's not a state secret, you know. Tell me about him."

"Look, Steve, I'm not trying to kick you out, but I have work to do. I just don't see why you need to know about my project." It was her project, after all.

"If that child has to be brought to the States from a war zone, then I need to know." Now his smile had developed an edge. "I also coordinate any military involvement in Children of the Day projects—which probably will mean getting that child out."

"Sorry." That didn't sound very gracious, did it? "I am sorry. I didn't realize that you were involved to such an extent."

He shrugged. "Now you know. So, are you ready to tell me about him now?"

"Of course." She managed a smile. "I don't know much yet. His name is Ali Tabiz, and he's five years old. He was referred to Children of the Day by a Dr. Mike Montgomery."

He nodded, his eyes intent as he studied the face on the screen. "I know Mike. If he wants our help, he has good reason."

"I suppose so, but he hasn't gotten back to us with much information on the boy's condition yet. It's apparently a heart problem that may need surgery. Oh, and we do know he's an orphan."

"Poor little guy." Steve reached out and touched the screen. "What do you say we send him a message?"

"A message? Well, I suppose we could ask Dr. Mike to tell him something."

"We can do better than that." He nodded to her desk chair. "If you'll let me use your computer for a minute, that is."

In an effort to seem more congenial, she slid out of the chair and watched as he started an e-mail. But the letters that appeared on the screen were Arabic.

Her mouth was probably hanging open in surprise. “How did you do that?”

He grinned. “All the computers here are equipped to switch to an Arabic alphabet. It’s necessary, given where the greatest need is at the moment.”

“But how do you know Arabic?” Steve seemed to be full of surprises.

He shrugged. “I have a knack for languages, I guess. And I was in the Middle East in an earlier offensive.”

“I didn’t know.”

An awkward silence followed, making her wonder what war had been like for a chaplain.

He frowned at the screen. “Since he’s only five, he’s probably not reading much yet, so let’s keep it simple and say we love him and want to see him.”

“That sounds good.” It did, and she was touched that Steve had thought of something that hadn’t even occurred to her.

“There we go.” Steve addressed it to the doctor’s e-mail address and hit Send. “Mike will see that he gets it and that somebody reads it to him.”

“I wish the doctor would get back to us. There’s not much more I can do until I hear from him.”

“You can trust Mike to do what’s right. We’ve worked with him before. He’s one of the good guys.”

She was beginning to think that Steve was one of the good guys, too. But that didn’t mean she wanted him taking over her job.

"I have a few more things to do before I go home, so if you don't mind—"

He nodded, getting up from the computer. "I know. It's your job, not mine."

"Well, yes, I guess that's what I mean. I'd like to show my new boss I can do it."

He stood watching her for a moment, and she almost thought there was a shadow of disappointment in his blue eyes.

"Not alone," he said. "Nobody around here is a solo act. It takes all of us to make this work."

"I'm sure cooperation is important, but—"

"But you're staff, while I'm just a volunteer?"

"I didn't mean that." She wasn't sure where this tension between them had come from.

He shrugged and started for the door, but before he reached it, he turned back toward her. "Keep me posted on Ali, will you?"

"All right."

He didn't seem convinced that she meant it. "Don't forget that I'm your military contact, Caitlyn. You'd better get used to working with me."

Chapter Three

Steve went in the side door of Children of the Day, hearing a hum of conversation from the lobby. Something must be going on, as it always was, but with a little luck he might be able to corner Anna for a private chat.

He had some information for her that might be helpful, but that wasn't his primary reason for turning up. The truth was that he was curious to see how Caitlyn was working out.

She'd been with COTD for all of two days, but if he knew Anna, that was plenty of time for her to come to a conclusion about Caitlyn.

He'd been bothered since their conversation about Ali. Maybe Caitlyn was dynamite at her position in New York, but Children of the Day ran on cooperation, lots of cooperation from all sorts of people. And Caitlyn had given off unmistakable vibes that she preferred to do everything all by herself.

Or maybe *he* was just the one person she didn't want to help her. That was always possible.

He tapped lightly on the French door to Anna's office.

It was standing ajar, as always, so that she could keep tabs on everything. With her passion and energy, it was no wonder the charity had grown from a small local effort to a world-respected organization in only five years.

He popped his head around the edge of the door. Anna was talking on the phone while staring intently at her computer screen, but at the sight of him, she smiled and waved him in.

In a moment she'd hung up the phone and turned her full attention to him. "Steve, how nice. I didn't expect to see you today."

"Well, since tomorrow's the Fourth of July, I thought I'd best come by today. Have you heard anything more from Dr. Mike?"

"No." Anna's brow furrowed. "I expected to by this time."

"I figured you might be concerned. The fact is that there's been a heavy offensive in Mike's area. I'd guess that's keeping him busy right now."

Anna's blue eyes filled with concern. "Is there fighting near his field hospital?"

He hesitated for a second, but Anna would guess the worst if he didn't level with her. "It sounds that way. It may be a day or two before things settle down."

"If they settle down." Anna rubbed at the line between her brows. "We both know how bad that can be. And that poor little boy. He could be right in the thick of things again."

He nodded. Anna was right—they did both know how bad war could be, especially on the innocent ones. "He's lost both his parents, and he's facing possible surgery. It seems like the kid ought to get a break soon."

"Well, he will if we can do anything about it." Anna's jaw tightened with her characteristic determination.

"Shall we pray for them?" He held out his hand, knowing her answer would be yes.

Anna nodded, putting her hand in his and closing her eyes.

"Dear Father, we know that You know better than we do what's happening right now with Mike and all those within his care, including little Ali. We ask that You surround them with Your love and protection and bring them through this trial to safety. Amen."

"Amen," Anna echoed. She released his hand. "Thank you, Steve."

He shrugged that off. "I should let you get back to business, but I did want to ask how Caitlyn's settling in. Is she working out all right?"

Anna's face lit with a smile. "As well as I knew she would the minute I met her. She's the kind of person you can just give a project and know she'll run with it."

"That's good." Although it didn't answer his main concern about her.

"It's just too bad she probably won't be staying in Prairie Springs for long."

He blinked, staring at Anna. "What do you mean? Did she tell you she's leaving?"

"Not in so many words." Anna shrugged. "But I can read between the lines as well as anyone. The most important thing in Caitlyn's life is her career, and that's back in New York. Obviously she's here to do her duty to her family, but I'd expect her to head back East just as soon as she can work things out."

"You're sure about that?" The question came out more sharply than it should.

She spread her hands. "I'd love to keep her, but I don't think that's going to happen."

Though he didn't say it out loud, he was appalled at the news.

How could Caitlyn even think of uprooting the girls? They needed the stability and security they had right here, among friends. And her mother, Betty, couldn't possibly manage by herself.

It sounded as if his concerns had been justified. It looked as if the bright, ambitious girl he'd once known had turned into a coldly driven career woman without any heart.

Caitlyn had forgotten how intensely Prairie Springs celebrated the Fourth of July, but it was certainly all coming back to her now. Texans were just naturally patriotic, and Texans living next to a military base doubled the patriotism. The twins were determined to enjoy every minute of the celebration, and so far, they seemed to be.

They'd already watched the parade and eaten their way through hot dogs and sweet corn and cherry pie, but at least they'd found a table near the river, where there was a bit of a breeze.

It had been a good day, but Caitlyn had to admit that the heat was getting to her. She'd thought New York in the summer was hot, but it was nothing compared to Texas. The heat hadn't bothered her that much as a kid, but now it was draining every bit of energy.

She pressed a paper cup of iced tea against her forehead, wishing she could just pour the tea over her head, as she watched the twins go around and around on the carousel. She smiled and waved to the girls as they passed her, thinking she and Carolyn had probably ridden those same painted wooden horses a long time ago.

Amanda was waving one arm like a rodeo rider as her palomino went up and down. Next to her, Josie clung to the pole of her stationary horse as if she feared it would throw her.

Worry flickered through her. Her mother felt Josie's timidity would resolve itself if they left her alone. Mama certainly had more experience than she did in dealing with children, so why did it still tease her, seeming to say she should do something?

The tempo of the carousel music changed, and the horses slowed their movement. The twins were out of her view, their horses now on the far side of the carousel.

Apprehension grabbed her. The carousel was going to stop with the twins about as far from her as they could be. Would they have sense enough to stay put until she reached them? She should have reminded them before the ride had started.

The music tinkled to a stop, and people began to pour off the carousel, even as others started to climb on. She struggled against the crowd of cheerful kids and adults, trying to spot the girls.

It was irrational, wasn't it, to feel so panicky because they were out of her sight? She couldn't seem to help it, and she couldn't get there fast enough.

Finally the crowd cleared, and she hurried past one painted horse after another. There was the palomino Amanda had ridden, with the stationary chestnut beside it. They were both empty.

She turned, searching the immediate area with her gaze.

Where were the children? They were her responsibility—she should have gone on the carousel with them. They could be scared—Josie might be crying.

And then she saw them walking toward her. Steve had each one by a hand, and Amanda was clutching a bunch of balloons.

She raced toward them, reaching them and catching both girls in a hug. "Where were you? I was scared when I couldn't find you."

Steve grasped her hand warmly. "They're fine. I'm sorry if they scared you."

"*Scared* is the right word." She took a breath. "What happened? Why didn't you stay where you were and wait for me to come?"

"I saw a man with balloons." Amanda's tone said she knew perfectly well she'd made a mistake and wasn't going to admit it.

"That's where I caught up with them," Steve said. "I happened to walk past the balloon man."

Caitlyn knelt so that she was eye to eye with the twins. "Listen, guys, you scared me. Don't ever do that again, okay?"

Amanda's lower lip came out, but after a moment she nodded. "Okay. I promise."

Josie nodded, too, looking close to tears.

"Good." Caitlyn hugged them. Had this been her first parenting success? At least Amanda hadn't argued. And thanks to Steve, they were safe.

She rose, blinking back a stray tear as she looked at Steve. "Thank you. If you hadn't seen them before they wandered even farther—"

"They wouldn't have gone far," he said comfortingly. He turned to the girls. "Hey, do you know how to make balloon animals?"

They shook their heads solemnly.

"Well, if I can just borrow a balloon, you'll see." He took one of the long balloons from Amanda's hand. "I wonder what I can make." He twisted the balloon in his hands, frowning a little. Finally he held it out.

"A giraffe." The twins shouted the word in unison.

He handed it to Josie, and she looked enchanted.

"One for me," Amanda said quickly. She gave him another balloon. "A giraffe, please."

"Well, we'll just have to see how it turns out." He twisted the balloon in his strong hands, frowning at it intently.

"What's wrong? Can't guarantee another giraffe?" Caitlyn asked softly.

He grinned. "I hate to promise what it's going to be. It usually looks like an animal, but not necessarily what I think it's going to be."

Fortunately for all of them, this one turned out enough like a giraffe to make Amanda happy, and the two girls decided to make their giraffes dance together to the music of the carousel.

"You're a success." Caitlyn smiled at him. "And we're lucky you came along when you did."

"Not so much luck," Steve said. "I ran into Betty and she asked me to join y'all for dessert and to watch the fireworks. I said I'd round you up."

"I see." It seemed she was destined to see Steve wherever she went. As he'd said, it was a small town. "Well, I'm still glad you came when you did. I was starting to panic. I'm beginning to appreciate every gray hair Carolyn and I caused our mother."

She said it lightly, but judging by Steve's expression, he wasn't taking it that way.

"Not easy being a parent, is it?"

"I'm not a parent. I can't ever take their mother's place."

The words came out without her thinking them through, but she realized they were true as soon as she said them. She'd do what she could, but she couldn't take Carolyn's place.

Steve stopped, turning to face her. "Is that really what you think?" He was frowning as if he'd taken her measure and found her lacking in some way. "Because that's what those children need, and you might just have to sacrifice what you want to give it to them."

Caitlyn could only stare at him in disbelief, as anger welled up in her at his stinging criticism. "I appreciate your interest, Chaplain Steve. But my family life is not really any of your business."

Without giving him a chance to respond, she grabbed the girls' hands and stalked off in the direction of the picnic grove.

It was all very well to have the last word, Caitlyn decided, but it lost its effect if you had to be with that person for another two hours.

She'd expected Steve to beg off watching the fireworks with them. That's what she'd have done, if their positions were reversed.

But he hadn't. He'd come back to the picnic table with them and eaten a slab of Mama's pecan pie and drunk a glass of lemonade, chatting all the while as if there weren't a trace of strain between them.

Now, he helped her spread a blanket at the riverbank—the ideal spot, her mother declared, for watching the fireworks.

"Thanks." She smoothed out a corner and sat down, glancing at the twins running among the blankets with a couple of friends, each one waving a flag or a glow stick. "Here's a spot for you, Mama." She patted the space next to her.

Her mother shook her head. "I was just talking to Maisie Elliot, and she's going on home now. I think maybe I'll ride along with her. I'm just a mite tired."

"Mama, if you're tired, we can go home now. We don't have to stay for the fireworks." She started to get up, but her mother was already shaking her head again.

"No, no, the girls would be so disappointed. You know how they've been looking forward to staying up for the fireworks. Y'all stay. Steve will keep you company, I know."

"I don't think—"

"I won't hear of you leaving," Mama said flatly. "Now just you do as I say, Caitlyn Ann."

"If a parent uses both names, you'd better give up," Steve said. His smile seemed genuine.

She sank back down reluctantly. "I guess you're right. We'll see you at home, then, Mama."

Her mother blew a kiss and started off to find her next-door neighbor. Caitlyn watched her go, and her heart clenched.

"She's aged," she said softly, nearly forgetting who she was talking to.

"It's been pretty rough on her." Steve leaned back on his elbows, his gaze intent on her face. "Even before Carolyn and Dean died, I could see the toll it was taking on her. She wouldn't admit it, but taking care of those girls full-time was beyond her."

"You think I don't know that?" She let the exasperation show in her voice. "Have you ever tried to stop Betty Villard from doing something she thought was her duty?"

"I know what you mean." He smiled. "Texas women are tough."

She shrugged. "I've been away too long to qualify, I'm afraid."

"Never say that." The laughter seemed to leave his face. "Caitlyn, I need to apologize to you for what I said earlier. I overstepped my bounds."

"Yes, you did."

"You're a hard case, you know that? I'm saying I'm sorry."

Much as she hated to admit it, that lopsided grin of his affected her. All the annoyance she'd been clinging to slid away.

"It's all right," she said. "I know you care about the girls. As for me—I'm still just feeling my way with them."

"It's pretty different from your life in New York, is it?"

"I'll say. I probably don't see a child from one month to the next there."

"No married friends with babies?"

She shrugged. "I work long hours. When I'm off, I guess I try to catch up on my sleep."

"That sounds a little lonely."

"Lonely? I don't have time to be lonely. The firm isn't happy unless they're getting sixty hours a week out of us."

He smiled. "Like I said. Lonely."

"You don't understand." He probably couldn't. She

didn't know what the army expected of a chaplain, but it couldn't be anything like the expectations of her firm. "That's what it takes in my line of work. You put in outrageous hours, knowing that the payoff at the end is worth it."

She sounded defensive, she realized. That was ridiculous. She didn't owe anyone an explanation of the life she'd chosen.

The military band struck up a march just then, and she was glad. It would save her from another argument with Steve.

"Hey, Amanda! Josie!" Steve called. "Come on, the fireworks are going to start any minute."

They came scurrying and dived onto the blanket. "I love fireworks," Amanda said. "They're my favorite thing next to chocolate cake and going to the movies."

"This girl's got her priorities straight." Steve scooped her onto his lap. "Look right out there over the water. Maybe you can be the first one to spot the fireworks."

Josie snuggled against Caitlyn. "I don't like the loud bang," she said confidingly. "I'm going to put my hands over my ears."

"That sounds like a good plan." Caitlyn patted her. "We'll hold on to each other, okay?"

"Okay."

The feel of that little body snuggled up against her was doing funny things to her heart. Lonely. Steve thought she'd been lonely.

She'd denied it, of course, but there might be a grain of truth in what he'd said. Maybe her life back in New York was a bit out of balance.

"There!" Amanda pointed to a dark rocket soaring upward. It exploded into a shower of white stars that arced downward toward their reflection in the water.

That was only the beginning. One rocket after another shot up to the oohs and aahs of the crowds along the riverbank. Amanda stared, mesmerized, and Josie alternated between watching and hiding her face in Caitlyn's lap.

Caitlyn smoothed Josie's fine, soft hair. She wouldn't have believed it a month ago, but it really was nice, sitting here, watching the awed looks on the children's faces.

As for Steve—she turned so she could see his strong profile, outlined against the water. It wasn't so bad having him here, either.

The last spectacular display seemed to go on and on as the band soared to a crescendo. Then, finally, the lights and sound faded away. It was over.

Before she could move or speak, she heard a sound drifting over the dark water, silencing the audience. It was a lone bugle, playing "Taps." The notes hung, sharp as crystal, in the still air.

Caitlyn's heart clenched painfully, and a tear trickled down her cheek. The sound was inexpressibly sad and beautiful.

The final notes died away, and for a moment nobody moved, nobody spoke. From somewhere in the crowd there was a muffled sob.

Then Steve pushed to his feet and moved to kneel next to her.

"She's asleep. I'll take her, if you can manage—"

He stopped. Then he reached out, wiping an errant tear from her cheek with one large, warm hand. Her gaze met his, and for a moment she couldn't think, couldn't breathe. Attraction twinkled between them, seeming as bright as the fireworks had been.

Then Steve sat back on his heels, looking startled. "I—"

he began, and seemed to lose his train of thought. He cleared his throat. "Sorry. I—I was saying that I'd carry Josie."

Amanda tugged at his pant leg. "I want you to carry me."

"But Aunt Caitlyn needs you," he said. "She has to have a strong girl to carry one end of the blanket."

Amanda's shoulders straightened. She'd be the strong one, obviously.

He slid his arms under the sleeping child, carefully not looking at Caitlyn. It didn't matter. She was aware of his every movement.

Was he as aware of her? Maybe it was better not to know. That flare of attraction—it was probably brought on by the emotion of the moment. It couldn't be anything else.

She stumbled to her feet, helping a tired Amanda gather up the blanket and then taking her tiny hand. It was definitely time to go home, and she would not feel regret. She wouldn't.

Chapter Four

Caitlyn's stomach clenched a little as she headed toward Anna's office. Being summoned like that in the hallowed halls of Graham, Graham and Welch was seldom a good thing. She hadn't been at Children of the Day long enough to know what it meant with Anna.

She did a rapid mental review of her work. Everything she could think to do regarding the Ali Tabiz situation had been done, and until they received the specifics from Dr. Mike she couldn't do anything more. Could she? She wasn't used to work situations in which the next step wasn't clear-cut, and that made her nervous.

She paused for just a second at the French doors, which stood ajar as usual, tapped lightly and went in. Anna was at her desk, talking, but she waved her in, never missing a beat. Anna obviously had multitasking down to a fine art, which was probably essential in running a foundation like this one.

"Here's Caitlyn now. Let's see what she has to say about it."

She went to the desk, realizing that Anna was talking

with someone via her webcam. Anna pulled a chair over so that they could sit next to each other, and Caitlyn slid into place.

"Dr. Mike, this is Caitlyn Villard, our new care coordinator. She's working on Ali's case. Caitlyn, this is Major Michael Montgomery, usually known as Dr. Mike."

"It's nice to meet you, Caitlyn. Glad to have you on board."

Even against the drab background of a cement-block wall, the man in scrubs had a vitality that transcended his obvious fatigue. His even features looked drawn, but his eyes sparkled with energy.

"It's good to meet you, as well, Dr. Mike. We've been hoping for some additional information on your young patient."

Dr. Mike grimaced. "I was sorry not to get back to you sooner. It's been pretty hot around here."

"We've been praying for you. But you're okay? And Ali?" Anna asked.

"Fine, fine." He glanced around, as if distracted. "I don't have much time, since people are lining up behind me to talk to their folks back home. I'm going to e-mail you a detailed medical report that you can share with the docs you normally use, so I'll just give you the main points now."

"Good." Caitlyn grabbed a pad from Anna's desk in the event he thought of anything that wouldn't be in the report.

"Ali was injured in the roadside bomb blast that killed his mother. At first glance his injuries seemed minor, but we soon realized his condition was more serious. A blow to the chest from the blast tore an abnormal opening between the two lower chambers of the heart—a ventricular septal tear. We've confirmed the diagnosis with an EKG and a sonogram, and I've consulted by phone with a cardiologist."

That sounded serious. Images of Amanda and Josie ran through her mind. "Will we need to schedule immediate surgery?" Caitlyn asked.

"Possibly not, but it's a tricky situation." His frown deepened. "The cardiologist feels that the tear could heal on its own. If so, he'll quickly regain his strength. But if it doesn't, if the heart begins to fail, the boy needs to be where he can have open heart surgery quickly."

"So we need to get him back here as soon as possible," Anna said.

"Right. There's just no place here that has either the equipment or the pediatric cardiac surgeons who can do the job."

"We'll do our best." Caitlyn scribbled rapid notes to herself. "How is he doing otherwise?"

"His other injuries were minor, fortunately. Of course he's grieving for his mother."

Her throat tightened. Like the twins, Ali was yet another child robbed of a mother's love by war.

"He's a cute kid." Dr. Mike's face creased in a tired smile. "Half the medical team has fallen for him already, and some of the chopper pilots have practically adopted him. We have to chase them out of his room so he can get enough rest."

"We'll make sure he gets plenty of attention here, too," Anna said. "Caitlyn will arrange for a complete workup with a pediatric cardiologist in Austin as soon as he arrives."

Caitlyn nodded. At least the child wouldn't have to have surgery the minute he got here. She'd gone over and over the process to have the army fly a foreign national to the United States for treatment. She didn't anticipate too much difficulty.

"What relative will accompany Ali to the U.S.?" Her pen was poised over the pad.

"None, unfortunately. He doesn't have a soul left over here."

"But..." She paused, her mind racing through all the regulations she'd read. "Legally I don't think we can bring a child who's a foreign national into the country without a guardian to give permission."

Anna's eyes clouded with concern. "We probably can't even get him out of there without it. Mike, you know the rules. There must be somebody who's willing to be responsible for the child—a distant cousin, an aunt or grandmother, anyone."

"Here's the thing." Dr. Mike leaned forward, as if he'd like to be in the room with them. "Ali's mother was married to an American serviceman who died when the boy was three. I'm still working on finding out all the details. The mother lived in a fairly remote village, and she probably used her family name for the child to protect him from discrimination."

"Are you sure they were actually married?" Anna asked the question Caitlyn had been thinking but hesitated to ask.

"I've seen the marriage certificate—it was with her things. The father's name was Gregory Willis." He shrugged. "So, the boy's an American citizen. That has to make a difference."

Caitlyn rubbed her temples, as if that might make her mind work a little faster. This was not the sort of legal issue that ever came up at her corporate practice in New York, and she certainly wasn't an expert on family or immigration law.

"Will you send us every bit of legal documentation you can find about the parents' marriage and the child's birth? I'm sure we're going to need it to prove that Ali is an American citizen." She at least knew that was the place to start.

"Will do." Mike glanced around. "Gotta go. I'll send everything I can ASAP. Good luck."

Before they could say goodbye, he was gone. Anna sat back in her chair, letting out a long breath. "Well. That's a new one."

"I was hoping you were going to say that COTD had dealt with a situation just like this before," Caitlyn said.

"No, I'm afraid this is uncharted territory. It looks as if you have your work cut out for you."

And while she was struggling to get up to speed, halfway around the world the clock might well be ticking for a small child who'd already lost far too much.

"Aren't we there yet, Aunt Caitlyn?" Amanda, in her booster seat in the back, kicked her feet against the driver's seat.

Caitlyn gritted her teeth, making a mental resolution to switch their seats so that Josie would be directly behind her. "Almost."

She glanced at the directions her mother had written out to the Fort Bonnell pool where the twins had swimming lessons. This was her first visit to the post, and it was far bigger than she'd realized. Everything about coming here seemed strange, including the stop she'd had to make at the visitors' center to pick up a pass even to drive onto the post.

She'd had to leave the Children of the Day offices just when she felt she was getting a handle on the search for

Ali's parentage, but her mother had a doctor's appointment this afternoon, and she'd promised to take the twins for their lesson.

"I'm going to swim underwater today," Amanda declared. "Hurry up, please."

"Me, too," Josie echoed.

She certainly wasn't going to "hurry up" beyond the speed limit, not with all these military types around. She passed a unit marching along the roadway, and a tank rumbled past her in the opposite direction.

She didn't think she'd ever seen so many uniforms in one place before. Funny that she'd never, so far as she remembered, come on the post when she was growing up in Prairie Springs.

Beige-colored buildings stretched down one straight street after another, seeming to go on and on as far as the horizon. Most of them bore signs in some sort of army shorthand that didn't mean a thing to her. Goodness, Fort Bonnell was a small city on its own, dwarfing Prairie Springs in comparison.

She passed the Fort Bonnell Christian Chapel on her right, one of her mother's landmarks. Steve's church. She'd called him there earlier, but he hadn't been in. She needed to involve him, as military liaison for COTD, in the search for Ali's father.

She'd confessed to Anna that she was totally out of her depth in dealing with the legal issues of the case. She hated feeling unprepared for any case she took on, but she had to be honest. Her legal background made her at least know the questions to ask, but not the answers.

Anna had been reassuring, referring her to a local

attorney, Jake Hopkins, who offered pro bono services to the charity. Unfortunately, Hopkins hadn't been in either when she'd called, so she'd left a detailed message on his machine, along with her cell phone number. Surely he'd be able to unscramble this. Maybe the answer was something perfectly simple.

She spotted the pool ahead and turned into the parking lot to cheers from the girls. She glanced at her watch. They were on time, but barely. She had a lot to learn about balancing work and kids. How did people do this every day?

She hustled the twins inside the fence, stripping off the sundresses that covered their swimsuits. Luckily Mama had gotten them ready. They'd been lathered with sunscreen and in their swimsuits, clutching towels, when Caitlyn arrived at the house.

She turned them over to the swimming teacher, a tanned young woman who seemed to have no difficulty controlling ten five-year-olds in a pool, and collapsed on a chaise under a beach umbrella with a sigh of relief.

She leaned back, closing her eyes. When Steve returned her call, it would be the first time they'd spoken since those intimate moments at the Fourth of July picnic. She'd been relieved not to run into him for a few days, wanting the perspective that a little time would give.

It had been one of those things, she'd decided. He was an attractive man, no one could deny that, with his intense gaze and easygoing grin. But she wasn't interested in him. That had been an illusion, brought on by the heightened emotions of the moment.

She was not going to think about him. She opened her

eyes and concentrated on the swim lesson. Predictably, Amanda was too bold and Josie too timid, but the teacher seemed to have them well in hand.

A shadow fell across her legs. She looked up, startled.

Steve. The jolt she felt when she saw him told her that those moments at the park had definitely not been an illusion.

"Hi. What are you doing here?"

"You called me, remember?" He dropped into the seat next to her, his face relaxing in that slightly crooked smile, his blue eyes warm.

Concentrate, she ordered herself. "I did call, but I didn't expect you to track me down. How did you know I'd be here?"

He shrugged. "I just took a chance that you'd be the one to bring the twins."

"But how did you know the twins had swimming lessons today?"

"I'm the one who set up the lessons. I thought it might be a good distraction for them."

She should have guessed, but she hadn't, and she was touched. "That was kind of you. Thank you."

Instinctively she reached out to him, and he took her hand in a warm, firm clasp. His touch seemed to travel along her skin, clear up her arm.

Quickly, she drew her hand away. "I…um, I needed to talk with you about the Ali Tabiz situation. We've heard from Dr. Mike."

"Yes, right. Ali." He seemed to have difficulty gathering his thoughts. "What did he say? Is the boy all right?"

"Yes, at the moment, but the injury to his heart is such that he could need surgery at any time, so we have to act quickly."

"Then we'll have to get moving. I'll check on flight space—"

"It's more complicated than the usual situation, it seems." She marshaled her thoughts. Focus on the job at hand, not on unwelcome attraction. "Ali doesn't have any relatives there to give him permission to come to the U.S. But Dr. Mike has found out that his father was an American soldier, so that should, I'd think, make it easier to get clearance."

He whistled softly. "That does put a different spin on the case, especially if the child doesn't have any family left there. Do you know what the legalities would be?"

"I don't know enough." She hated admitting it. "Anna referred me to a local attorney who has helped the foundation in the past with immigration issues, so I have a call in to him."

"Jake Hopkins." He nodded. "I know him. Ex-military. He'll do a good job for you. Well, obviously we'll need information about the father, so I can start on that end of it through military channels. Do you have a name?"

"Yes. It's Gregory Willis. Dr. Mike is sending a copy of the mother's marriage license, so that will give us some documentation, at least."

She glanced at Steve, sensing a lessening of his attention. He was frowning slightly, his gaze seeming to turn inward.

"What's wrong?"

He jerked back to attention and shook his head. "Nothing. The name seemed vaguely familiar, that's all. Do we have any other information on the man—rank, dates of birth and death, his unit?"

"Not that I know of, but Dr. Mike promised to keep looking." Was she imagining it, or did Steve seem to know more than he was letting on? "So you think you might have known him?"

"I didn't say that." He stood, his tall figure blocking the sun. "I'll get right on it and call you later."

He turned and quickly walked away, leaving her vaguely dissatisfied. There had been something that seemed out of place in his reaction to the name.

Still, Steve knew how crucial this was and it was his insistence that they cooperate and work together. If he knew anything about Gregory Willis, he'd tell her. Wouldn't he?

"So you're Paul Windham's son." Retired General Marlon Willis—tall, erect, white-haired—eyed Steve up and down as if he were inspecting the troops. He wore western dress, his hat tossed onto the antlers that were mounted over his desk, but he was every inch military.

Steve nodded, glad he'd come in uniform to see Gregory Willis's father. "Yes, sir. My daddy mentioned you often."

"Good man, that. I hope he's well."

"Doing fine, sir. He and my mother retired to Wyoming."

He'd hoped the fact that his father had once known General Willis would ease his entry to the gracious Georgian house in Prairie Springs's historic district, and it had. The maid had shown him directly to the study where the general sat in a leather armchair with his newspaper.

The bookshelf-lined room was filled with military memorabilia dotting the walls and adorning the shelves.

One thing seemed to be missing. There were no photos of Captain Gregory Willis, the general's only child, killed in action two years ago. Gossip had it the general had been devastated by Greg's death. That could make this much more difficult.

"What brings you here today, Chaplain?" Willis apparently felt the niceties had been observed sufficiently.

Steve took a breath, sending up a silent prayer for guidance. "I'd like to talk with you about your son, Gregory."

The elderly man froze, his hands tightening on the arms of his leather chair. For a long moment he didn't speak, but a muscle in his jaw twitched, and his face began to redden.

"I don't speak of him." He grated the words out, standing. "If that's all—"

"I'm sorry, sir." Steve rose, too. "I'm afraid this is important."

Willis's face reddened alarmingly. "I said I don't talk about him."

This was even worse than he'd expected, but he knew that people reacted differently to grief. "I'm very sorry for your loss, sir."

"Thank you," he said, clearly ending the conversation. "I'll see you out." Willis turned toward the door.

He couldn't let the man shove him away before he'd said what he'd come to say.

"I've been working with Children of the Day to arrange medical treatment for a five-year-old boy named Ali Tabiz. I'm sure you know of their work."

The general jerked a short nod. He wasn't making this easy, but at least he hadn't thrown Steve out.

"The child was injured in a bombing that killed his mother, who was apparently his only living relative. But we've learned that the mother was married to an American soldier. Captain Gregory Willis. Your son."

Was he wise to come right out with it? He wasn't sure, but the old soldier seemed like the type who'd prefer straight talking.

"No." The general ground out the word.

He was taken aback at the flat denial. "I'm sorry, sir, but I've looked into it very thoroughly. There seems no doubt that Gregory married this woman—"

"That may be." A vein throbbed in his temple. "But he's not my son."

"If you mean it's another Gregory Willis," he began, but the general silenced him with a sharp gesture.

"I mean Gregory is not my son. I cut him off when he made that foolish marriage. I'm sorry the woman is dead, but it's no concern of mine."

For a moment he couldn't say anything. He knew better than to take the general's brusque words at face value. There was a world of pain, grief and anger beneath them, and he sent up a silent prayer for guidance.

"Gregory had a son," he said gently. "Ali. He's five now, and he has suffered a serious injury to his heart. If we don't bring him to the States for surgery, he could die."

"Then do it." He turned toward the window, the sunlight gleaming from his white hair and reflecting off the ornate buckle of his belt. "That's what that charity does, isn't it?"

"Children of the Day is working on the case, but it's more complicated than most. The boy has no relatives left there to make decisions for him. But you are his grandfather, and if you got involved—"

"No!" He swung back toward Steve, his face such an alarming shade of red that Steve feared for his health.

"Gregory made his decision, and I made mine. That child is no kin of mine."

"He's your flesh and blood, whether you want to claim him or not." Anger wasn't going to help. Steve pushed down the rising tide of indignation. "If you don't help him, the boy could die."

General Willis stood looking out the window for a few minutes, but Steve doubted that he was seeing the quiet gardens beyond the window.

Finally he turned back, his face rigid. "You say the child needs surgery. How bad is it?"

"He may need surgery," Steve corrected. "The blast that killed his mother tore a hole between the chambers of his heart. The doctors say there's a chance that it will heal naturally, but if it doesn't, he has to be where he can receive immediate open heart surgery. That's why we want to bring him here."

If his words touched the gruff old man, he didn't give any sign of it. "Very well." His voice grated on the words. "I'm not accepting any responsibility, but I suppose I should do something. You can count on me for whatever financial resources are needed."

"That's very generous." He said the words politely, when what he wanted to do was grab the man, shake him and force him to see that this was Greg's son they were talking about.

But he knew his limitations. He couldn't change the general's heart. Only God could do that.

"This is between us, understand? I don't want my name brought into it." The general pointed a finger at him. "No word of my help gets out to anyone."

Caitlyn's face formed in Steve's mind. "The caseworker from Children of the Day will have to be told."

"No!" His fist thudded the nearest lamp table for emphasis, and the brass lamp rocked dangerously. "No one knows I'm involved. Those are my conditions. Take it or leave it."

A thousand arguments flooded his mind, but he choked them back. Now wasn't the time to argue. Maybe, after the general had a chance to think about this, he'd be more amenable.

So he'd take the offer, because that was the only possibility at the moment, and at least it left an avenue open for further conversation about the child.

"All right. I'll do it the way you want it."

The general strode quickly to the door and threw it open. "I don't want to hear about this ever again, understand? Just let me know when money is needed, and I'll write a check. But I don't want to discuss this situation ever." He nodded toward the hallway. "Good day."

Steve walked out, his mind churning. Had he handled it in the right way? Impossible to know. The general's reaction could have been the same no matter how he was approached or by whom.

Lord, if I've messed this up, I'm sorry. I'm asking You to work on him, because it looks like he won't listen to anything else from me.

He headed for his car, his mind on the other problem this situation raised. How was he going to work with Caitlyn without betraying the general's secret? He didn't have an answer to that.

Chapter Five

"Amanda, slow down."

Josie clung to Caitlyn's hand as they walked down the long hallway in the church's educational wing, but Amanda had darted ahead, and she didn't respond to the sound of Caitlyn's voice.

"Amanda!"

This time Amanda did slow a bit, looking back over her shoulder at her aunt. For an instant Caitlyn felt as if she and Carolyn were on their way to a Sunday-school class again, with Carolyn running ahead as she always did, then darting that impish look at her sister, daring her to run, too.

She glanced into one of the rooms as she passed, trying to push the image of her sister out of her mind. It refused to go.

Carolyn had always been the daring one, and following her had inevitably led to mischief. Older by two years, Caitlyn should have known better, but too often, she'd been the one who'd had to get Carolyn out of trouble.

The Sunday-school rooms had been repainted and refurnished since their day, of course, but the rooms still seemed familiar, with their pictures of Jesus and their low tables and child-size chairs.

She and Carolyn had been in church school faithfully every Sunday morning. They'd sung in the children's choir and participated in the pageants. But that was a long time ago.

Amanda skipped back down the hall to them and grabbed Josie's hand, tugging at her. "Come on, slowpoke. Run with me, pokey slow, pokey slow."

Josie leaned against Caitlyn's leg. "Manda's teasing me, Auntie Caitlyn. Make her stop."

She wasn't sure which bothered her more—Amanda's naughtiness or Josie's whining. "Both of you stop fussing. Amanda, where is…" She paused, not sure she wanted to use the words *grief center* to a child. "Where is Mrs. Olga's room?"

"Around the corner." Amanda pointed, and then dashed off again. "I'll beat you," she shouted, her voice echoing from the block walls.

Caitlyn's nerves tightened. The situation with the girls seemed to slide further out of her control with every passing day.

Back in New York, when she'd first heard the news, she'd been grief-stricken. But she'd thought the task ahead of her would be fairly simple.

Now she wasn't so sure. She worried about her mother's well-being, worried about succeeding at her new job, and most of all worried about helping the twins deal with their grief. Perhaps Mrs. Terenkov, Anna's mother, would be able to give her some guidance.

She rounded the corner just in time to see Amanda crash straight into a woman emerging from one of the rooms.

"Amanda!" She hurried to them, but luckily the woman was laughing, bending to catch Amanda in a hug.

"Manda, Manda, always in a hurry." The woman spun toward them, catching Josie up in an equally enthusiastic hug. "And here's my Josie-bug. How are you today?"

"I bumped my elbow." Josie solemnly displayed a chubby elbow with not a mark on it, which the woman kissed with an extravagant smack.

"There you are, my darling." She ruffled Josie's bangs and then turned to Caitlyn. "And you are Caitlyn, of course. I've heard of you from my Anna." Caitlyn found herself also enveloped in a hug.

Before she could figure out how to respond to this display of affection from someone she'd never met, Mrs. Terenkov had turned back to the children, chattering away to them as easily as if she were another five-year-old.

Caitlyn gave herself a mental shake. She'd expected an older version of Anna, if she'd thought of it at all. True, the family resemblance was strong, with Olga having the same snapping blue eyes and blond hair, the same quick movements.

But there the similarity ended. Anna was businesslike, perhaps a little reserved, a bit formal and serious. Olga bubbled with life, laughing, gesturing, chattering away with her faint Russian accent decorated with Texasisms. She wore a long denim skirt, its belt sporting an oversize silver buckle embossed with a longhorn steer, and a colorful embroidered blouse.

"In you go." Olga shooed the twins through a door decorated with balloons, as if for a party.

This was a grief-counseling center? Caitlyn peered into

a cheerful playroom, its walls adorned with murals of Bible scenes, all of them featuring children, except for one wall taken up by an overflowing bulletin board, labeled Wall of Hope.

Several children were already in the room, pulling puzzles and games from the shelves, and the twins ran to join them, with Amanda shouting, of course.

"So, Caitlyn, what do you think of my little haven?" Olga's expression was shrewd, as if she guessed at Caitlyn's doubts.

"It's very cheerful." Her gaze lingered on the children. "I didn't realize there would be so many kids needing grief counseling."

Olga's gaze softened as she looked at her little flock. "There will be more still to come, I'm afraid. We've had many losses."

"But—does the surviving spouse usually stay here in Prairie Springs?" She'd think they'd want to move close to family, rather than staying near the army post, with all its reminders.

"Gold Star families can stay on post for another six months after their loss. Many choose to do that." She smiled at Caitlyn's expression. "You are thinking that you would want to get away."

"I guess I am."

"But you see, here they have support. They have other army spouses who understand what they're going through. It can ease the adjustment for them."

That made a lot of sense. In spite of her slightly outrageous air, Olga seemed to have a solid core of warmth and common sense.

"So you usually have the children for about six months?"

She nodded. "The twins, of course, I hope will be around longer."

"How are they doing? Really?" She asked the question she'd been longing to ask.

Olga shrugged. "It's early yet. So far they are not talking much about their loss. I'm hoping our Adopt a Soldier program will help them open up."

"Adopt a Soldier?"

"Each child picks a deployed soldier to correspond with. They seem—"

"I don't think so." Everything in her recoiled at the thought. "The twins have just lost both of their parents over there. I don't think it's a good idea for them to get attached to someone else who's in danger."

"No?" Olga shrugged. "Well, I must start. We can talk about it when you pick them up." She stepped into the room and began to close the door.

"I thought I would stay—" she began.

"Sorry, no visitors." Olga closed the door firmly, leaving Caitlyn staring at it.

Steve stepped out of Pastor Franklin Fields's office and stopped dead in his tracks. He knew the twins came to the church for the grief support group, of course, but he'd forgotten it was today. Otherwise, he might have arranged his visit with Frank for another time.

Avoiding Caitlyn was not a solution to his problem. He knew that as well as anyone, but still, he dreaded talking to her with the memory of his visit to General Willis fresh in his mind.

Actually, Caitlyn looked a tad disconcerted at the sight of him, too. She hesitated for a second and then strode down the hall toward him as if she were hurrying down Fifth Avenue, or wherever she hung out in New York City.

"Hey, there, Caitlyn," he said, trying to sound casual. "Dropping the girls off, are you?"

She gave a quick nod, her face clouding for an instant, as if something about that bothered her. "I didn't expect to see you here."

"Pastor Fields and I had to talk about a few projects we have going on. Have you met yet?"

She shook her head, looking up as a tall figure emerged from the office behind him.

He stepped clear of the door in order to make the introductions. "Caitlyn, this is Reverend Franklin Fields. Frank, Caitlyn Villard, Betty's daughter."

"How nice it is to meet you." Frank's hand enveloped Caitlyn's. "Betty's a very valued part of our church family."

Caitlyn murmured something conventional in response. She probably found Frank a little intimidating at first glance, as most people did, given his height, his composure and his iron jaw. It'd be a shame if she didn't look beyond the stone wall of Frank's exterior to the warm, compassionate human being he really was.

"Well, I must be going." As usual, Frank was on his way to his next responsibility. Small talk wasn't his strong suit. "I look forward to seeing you at worship on Sunday, Caitlyn." He strode off down the hall.

Steve caught a faintly disconcerted look on Caitlyn's face as she looked after him. "What's wrong? Weren't you planning to go to church this week?"

Now the look turned annoyed as she glanced at him. "I'm sure I will. My mother always attends."

Something about the way she phrased that made his eyebrow lift. "And you're not in the habit?"

"I didn't say that. I suppose since I've been away—" She stopped, as if deciding he didn't need to hear the rest of that sentence.

He thought he could fill it in, in any event. Caitlyn had drifted away from church as she'd drifted away from her family. What would it take to bring her back?

She turned, looking down the hallway toward the rooms that the church had devoted to the grief center. They included the children's playroom, an adult meeting room and Olga's small, overcrowded office.

"What do you know about Olga—Mrs. Terenkov?" Caitlyn asked abruptly.

"You may as well say Olga. She's on a first-name basis with everyone in town, to say nothing of half the state of Texas."

"Olga, then. She's a little..." Caitlyn paused, as if searching for the right word.

"Overwhelming? Enthusiastic? Outrageous?" he suggested.

Her face relaxed. "All three. But is she really qualified as a counselor?"

"Her credentials are hanging on her office wall, if you want to read them. Of course, some of them are in Russian, so that might make it difficult. I could translate, if you like."

"Very funny." She frowned slightly. "I'm just concerned about the twins. That's all. Olga mentioned something about her Adopt a Soldier program. I'm not sure it's a good idea for Amanda and Josie. Won't it just remind them of their own loss?"

It was the first time she'd seemed to defer to his opinion, and he felt a strong desire to take away the worried look from her face.

"I don't suppose there's anything that wouldn't remind them of that, do you?" he asked gently. "I understand Olga has found it a good way to get the children talking about their loss, and talking is the first step toward healing."

He believed what he was saying. Of course he did. So why was it he'd never found it possible to talk about his own loss?

He shoved that thought away. This was about Caitlyn and her nieces, not about him.

"You may be right. This is uncharted territory for me." But Caitlyn's hazel eyes were still clouded with worry.

Instinctively, he touched her hand in a moment of sympathy, and again felt the current of energy that flowed between them. She looked up, her eyes darkening a little.

He cleared his throat, trying to focus. "Why don't you talk to the twins about the program? Just see how they feel about it. I wouldn't push them to participate if they don't want to."

She nodded, taking a step back as if she'd decided they were standing a little too close. "That's a good idea. Thank you."

"Anytime."

She nodded again, and he could almost see her change mental gears. "By the way, I'd hoped to get in touch with you today or tomorrow. How is the search for Ali's relatives going?"

He pasted a smile on his face and trusted she wouldn't

realize how phony it was. "I'm making some progress, but I don't have anything definite yet."

At least, he hoped it could be described as progress. He was on the trail of a friend of Gregory Willis's, who might be able to shed some light on the rift between the general and his son.

She frowned a little. "I'd hoped to be further along than this by now. I'm meeting with Jake Hopkins this afternoon after I drop the children at home. He's going to brief me on Texas law as it pertains to this situation."

"You can count on Jake. And just so you won't think I'm lying down on the job, I do have one bit of good news. I have an anonymous donor who's willing to put up whatever funds are needed for Ali's trip and his care."

"Really?" Her face lit with pleasure. "That's wonderful. Who is it?"

He grinned. "You do know what anonymous means, don't you?"

"Well, I can understand someone not wanting publicity about their generosity, but surely COTD can be trusted with his or her identity."

"Sorry." He could imagine the general's reaction to Steve's breaking his promise, to say nothing of his own guilt if he did such a thing. "You have your attorney-client confidentiality, and I have the bond of secrecy between a pastor and his flock."

"It's someone in the military, then?"

"Nice try, Counselor. I'm not talking."

She looked ready to pursue the subject, so he took a quick step away. "I have to head out. I'll check in with you as soon as I have something, all right?"

He didn't give her a chance to answer, just continued down the hall.

Keeping secrets was part of his job, but it had never bothered him as much as it did right now. And he guessed that was a measure of how much Caitlyn Villard affected him.

"Thanks so much for fitting me in today." Caitlyn followed Jake Hopkins from the outer reception area, empty now since his secretary must have gone home, and into his inner office.

"No problem." That slow Texas drawl told her Jake was a native. He was also tall, tanned and casual—his white shirt was rolled to the elbows, and if he'd started the day with a tie, it wasn't in evidence now.

He limped to the wide desk, seeming to lean heavily on the wooden walking stick he used, and settled into the leather chair behind it, waving to a pair of matched client's chairs that faced the desk.

One of the black leather chairs was already occupied by a bad-tempered-looking orange cat. Caitlyn chose the opposite one.

"Anna tells me you do a great deal of pro bono work for the foundation."

And hopefully he was about to do a bit more. If he'd found a simple process for getting Ali cleared to come to the States, she'd be eternally grateful.

He nodded. "Glad to help out any way I can. Those folks do a Texas-size job of dealing with the woes of the world."

"Yes, they do."

"It sure seems like you're a big asset to them, according to Anna. Lucky for them you came back to Prairie Springs, though I'm sorry for the reason."

"Thank you." She was resigned by this time to the fact that everyone in town seemed to know about her return and Carolyn's and Dean's deaths.

He quirked an eyebrow. "You thinkin' about getting licensed in Texas, now that you're here? Wouldn't be tough at all, you know."

Just thinking about applying to the bar in Texas set her nerves on end. That would be admitting she'd be here for the foreseeable future.

"I'm not planning on that at the moment." She managed a smile. "Have you come up with anything helpful about our little patient?"

Jake leaned forward, elbows on the desk, and linked his fingers together. "I had to do some searching, I confess. This situation hasn't come up in my practice before, but I think I've got it taped now."

"Great."

Well, it wasn't really great as far as she was concerned, because it meant admitting that she had to rely on someone else. Caitlyn flipped open her notebook. But at least the conversation was safely away from the subject of her future.

"First off, is there any question of the boy's legitimacy?"

"Apparently not, as far as we can tell. Dr. Montgomery found Ali's mother's marriage license among her belongings after her death." She drew out the copy Dr. Mike had sent and handed it to him. "We felt that the original should stay with the boy."

"Wise precaution." He looked over the form, nodding. "Now, I assume you also have the boy's birth certificate and a record of his registration as a U.S. citizen born in a foreign country."

"Registration?" She sounded blank. She hated that.

"The father should have registered his birth at an American consulate as soon as possible after the boy's birth. Do you know if that was done?"

"I've no idea." And how difficult might it be, tracking down the birth of one child in a war-torn country? "I'll get going on finding the documentation. It has to be somewhere."

"Once you have proof of that, the rest should fall into place," Jake said. "Now, the next thing we need is a relative of the father who's willing to petition the court for a managing conservatorship."

"Not a guardianship?"

He shook his head. "That would be much more complicated, and since time is of the essence, we'll get the boy here faster this way. The relative agrees to assume responsibility, I explain to the judge that this is a medical emergency, and we're off and running. Who is the relative?"

"We don't have one yet." They should have. Why hadn't Steve come up with anything? "I'm working on it with Chaplain Steve Windham."

"Steve knows his way around army red tape. He'll find someone in no time." Jake shoved his chair back. "Just you call me as soon as you have a willing relative, and we can have it done in no time at all."

"All right, I'll do that." Given how confident Jake was, it was a wonder that Steve hadn't found a relative already. "And thanks again for your help."

"My pleasure." Jake shook hands, leaning on the desk for support. "And when you decide to get yourself licensed in Texas, you just let me know and I'll walk you through the procedure."

"Thank you." She didn't expect to take him up on that, but it was nice of him to offer. She slipped her notebook into her bag and then paused. "One more thing, Jake. What if we can't find a willing relative?"

He shook his head. "I'm not saying we couldn't get things straightened out eventually. Trouble is, if his medical condition goes bad, it might not be in time."

His words set up an echo in her heart. She seemed to see again that thin face, those big dark eyes.

"We'll find someone."

I promise, she said silently to the wistful little boy. *I promise.*

So that meant she had to get Steve moving on this. Either that, or figure out a way to do it herself.

Chapter Six

Caitlyn grappled with the difficulties presented by Ali's case as she drove back to the house. The time factor was what she feared most.

It wasn't that she hadn't dealt with tough deadlines before, but those had been with business cases and liability suits. Now it was a child's life hanging in the balance.

That single fact was paralyzing her. Her normal working life was structured exactly the way she wanted it, with no personal emotions to risk.

She pulled into the driveway and moved through the heat to the house. It had been a stifling day, and Mama's flowers drooped dispiritedly against the porch. If only it would rain. She glanced up at the cloudless sky. That didn't seem likely.

She hurried into the house, already accustomed, in the few weeks she'd been home, to the welcoming aroma of dinner cooking. But today she didn't smell a thing.

Puzzled, she followed the sound of children's voices into the family room that adjoined the kitchen. The twins were watching a video that seemed to feature singing animated vegetables, and Mama lay back in her recliner, eyes closed.

Caitlyn's heart lurched. "Mama, what's wrong? Are you sick?"

The twins turned around at the sound of her voice, and her mother opened her eyes.

"Grammy has a headache," Amanda said. "So we're keeping quiet and being very good."

"That's nice of you." Caitlyn turned from the twins to her mother. "Mama, are you okay?"

"I'm fine, fine." Her mother glanced at the clock. "Goodness, look at the time. I'd best be getting supper on."

The exhaustion in her mother's face frightened Caitlyn. Her mom never admitted weakness, and if she was sick, no one heard about it.

"You'll do nothing of the kind. You sit right there and tell me what's wrong. Supper can wait."

Her mother put one hand to her forehead. "Just foolish, I guess, running around in this heat trying to get some errands done after my checkup. It gave me a headache."

"You look exhausted." Why hadn't she noticed that earlier?

Mama shrugged. "I didn't sleep very well last night. Josie was up with a nightmare, and afterward, I couldn't seem to doze off again."

And she had slept right through it. Guilt was a weight on her shoulders.

"Mama, you're doing too much, that's all." And she was supposed to be helping. "From now on, the monitor goes in my room."

The twins insisted they were too big to have a baby monitor in their room at night, but her mother had put one in from the time they came to live with her anyway, just to ensure that she always heard them.

"You need your rest—" Mama began, but Caitlyn cut her off.

"No arguments. From now on, I'll be in charge of the middle-of-the-night events. Now, you go right on up to your bedroom and have a rest. I'll take care of supper and the girls."

To her astonishment, her mother didn't argue. Instead she nodded. "Maybe I will, at that. But you call me if you need me."

"I won't." Caitlyn pressed her cheek against her mother's. "Go on now."

Her mother headed up the steps, detouring to the freezer to take out an ice pack. The twins turned back to their video.

Caitlyn looked around the kitchen, hoping for inspiration. With the hours she usually worked, she rarely cooked. She could make a terrific crab omelet, her special brunch dish, but she didn't suppose the five-year-olds would go for that.

Just when she'd found a package of macaroni and cheese, the telephone rang.

"Hi, Caitlyn, how is small-town life treating you? Are you ready to come back to us yet?"

Longing swept through her at the sound of Julia Maitland's voice, her best friend since college. They still saw each other in New York at least once a week, despite the fact that their careers had gone in different directions, with her friend now a buyer for a department-store chain.

Julia was always trying to get Caitlyn into something other than what she called her lawyer suits.

"I wish I were." She glanced at the twins and felt faintly guilty again. Did she really wish that? "What's going on with you?"

"Nothing too exciting. Everyone heads out of the city on the weekends in July, you know that. Or else takes off on a long vacation. Seriously, how are you? I'm sure it's been rough."

"Okay, I guess. There's still a lot to do here with the family. And I did take a part-time job, just to have some money coming in."

"I know how that is. But listen, I just might have a solution to that part of your problem. You remember my cousin Becky?"

Caitlyn scoured her memory. "The one who wants to be an actress?"

"That's her. Well, her parents are funding her for six months in the city to see if she can make it. Becky needs a place to stay, obviously, and I thought of you right away. Would you consider subletting your place?"

Instantly her mind began ticking off advantages and disadvantages. Subletting would solve her money problems for the moment, at least. But it would also mean admitting that she was losing the life that she loved. Everything in her rebelled at that thought.

"I don't know," she began, and then turned at the sound of battle in the family room. "I have to go, Jules. The twins have started World War Three in the next room. How soon do you have to have an answer?"

"I can't give you more than a week, I'm afraid." Julia's

tone grew serious. "You know I'd much rather have you back here than my cousin any day, but it sounds as if you're needed there."

"At the moment, anyway. I'll call you soon with an answer."

She hung up and strode into the family room, forcibly separating the twins. "What is going on? Couldn't you see I was on the phone?"

"Manda called me a baby," Josie wailed. "I'm not a baby just 'cause I had a nightmare."

"No, of course you're not. Everyone has nightmares sometimes."

"Well, she hit me." Amanda sniffed, as if trying to produce tears. "And you're not s'posed to hit, no matter what."

"No, you're not," she agreed, wondering how her mother had dealt with this for six months.

"Listen, since Grammy doesn't feel good, why don't you come and help me with the supper? We'll make some macaroni and cheese and fruit salad."

"Yaaay," they chorused. Turning off their tears in an instant, the twins raced for the kitchen.

Caitlyn followed more slowly. Maybe she had to apply more of her legal-negotiating skills to dealing with the twins.

In a few minutes the girls were deeply engrossed in adding fruit to the salad. With the macaroni cooking, Caitlyn leaned on the counter, watching them.

Amanda's eyes sparkled. She waved a wooden spoon while Josie counted blueberries solemnly into a bowl.

"Hurry up, hurry up," she chanted, and Josie pouted.

Eager to avoid another battle, Caitlyn sought for a change of subject. "Did you have a good time with Mrs. Olga today?"

They nodded. "Mrs. Olga's nice. We do fun games," Amanda said.

"And we made pictures to send to some soldiers," Josie added.

That sounded like part of the Adopt a Soldier program, and she thought of Steve's advice. *Talk to them about it.*

Her stomach clenched. It would be the first time she'd brought up anything that might touch upon their parents' deaths, but she had to deal with it. She wouldn't pass it off to Mama.

"Mrs. Olga told me about how you might adopt a soldier from Fort Bonnell who's overseas," she said cautiously. "You could write to him or her and send pictures, and they'd write back. Do you think you'd like to do that? You don't have to if you don't want to."

"We want to," Amanda announced. "Lots of kids do that. It's fun. They get letters and pictures back, and even e-mails. Can we get e-mails on your computer, Auntie Caitlyn?"

"I suppose." She focused on her other niece. "What about you, Josie?"

Josie nodded slowly. "I told Mrs. Olga maybe we could have two soldiers who were married to each other." Her voice dropped to a whisper. "That would be sort of like Mommy and Daddy."

Her heart seemed to be shredding into tiny pieces. "Do you think that might make you feel sad?" Her voice sounded choked.

"Maybe a little bit," Amanda said. "But it would be nice, too."

Josie nodded, her face serious. "I think Mommy would like us to do it."

Caitlyn fought back tears as panic rippled through her. She wanted to race back to New York, to pick up again a life where nothing tore her heart to shreds on a daily basis.

But she couldn't.

"Okay." She managed a smile. "I guess we'll ask Mrs. Olga to find us a couple of soldiers to adopt."

And pray this was the right decision. She paused, startled at her thought. Pray? When had she started thinking of that as the first course of action? Maybe she'd been around Chaplain Steve too much.

Steve sat at his desk, staring at the computer screen. But he wasn't working, he was praying.

Lord, please, show me the way out of this situation. I thought I was doing the right thing by approaching Willis alone. Or was I being proud, thinking I was the only one who could do it? That's just what I believe Caitlyn does, but I'm the guilty one this time.

And now he was stuck, unable to tell her about the general, unable to show Marlon Willis that his lack of forgiveness hurt both him and an innocent child.

He buried his face in his hands.

Please, Father, forgive me. Show me how to make this right without breaking faith with anyone, most of all with You.

A rap on the door jerked him back into the moment. *In Jesus' name, Amen.*

"Come in."

The words were barely out of his mouth when the door flew open. One look at Caitlyn's face told him something had happened. Almost without thinking, he got to his feet and held out his hand to her.

"Caitlyn, what is it? What's wrong?"

"Wrong? I don't know how you can ask me that."

She'd found out about the general. That had to be it. She'd found out, and she was furious with him. Justifiably so.

He uttered a silent, wordless prayer for guidance. "I take it you know about Greg Willis's family. How did you find out?"

Her eyes sparked fire. "I should have found out from you."

"Yes. You should have."

His words didn't seem to blunt her anger, but perhaps they deflected it a little.

Her jaw tightened, as if to hold back a hasty response. "I hadn't heard from you, so I used some of COTD's contacts to look into Gregory Willis. They found General Willis in a matter of hours, right here in town. If they could do it, you obviously did, too."

He nodded. "Yes. I did."

"Why didn't you tell me? Were you trying to make me fail?"

"No!" That was the last thing he'd have her believe. "Caitlyn, you can't believe that."

"Then tell me what to think. Why did you keep this a secret? You knew from the moment I told you at the pool, didn't you?"

"I didn't. Caitlyn, you have to trust me on that. I vaguely remembered General Willis as a friend of my father, that's all, and I knew he had a son. It wasn't until I looked into it further that I found out the son was the Gregory Willis we were looking for."

"And you didn't tell me."

How could he explain this so that she'd understand? "I

knew Marlon Willis had a reputation as a crusty old guy who didn't like interference from anyone. I thought his friendship with my father might ease the way if I went to see him alone."

"And did it?" She didn't look as if she'd forgiven him, but at least she was listening.

"Not really." He sighed. "Caitlyn, I'm sorry. I can't divulge what he said to me. Just take my word for it—we're not going to get anywhere with the general."

"I gather he's your anonymous donor." She took a few steps across the office, as if she couldn't stand still any longer. "Never mind, you don't have to tell me."

"We'll have to go on without him. We'll find another way—"

"We can't," she said flatly. "I met with Jake Hopkins. He says we have to have a relative who will agree to take on legal responsibility for the boy before we can bring him to the States."

That hit him hard. "I'm sorry. I didn't know. If I talk with General Willis again—"

"No. You've done enough. This time I'll talk with him."

It was what he expected her to say, but he had to dissuade her. "You don't know what you're getting into. Please, let me."

She shook her head decisively. "No, thanks. I'll do it myself."

"That's your way of dealing with everything, isn't it?" The words were out without thought, and he instantly regretted them.

She stiffened. "Funny, this time you were the one who did that." Turning, she stormed out of the office, slamming the door.

* * *

Caitlyn exited General Willis's house into a pounding rainstorm. Appropriate, since she felt as if she'd just been put through a wringer.

She paused on the front step to put up her umbrella. It was pouring so hard she could barely see her car, parked at the bend of the circular driveway, but if she lingered any longer she was afraid the general would come out to chase her off his property, maybe with one of the guns he had mounted in his study. He certainly seemed capable of it.

Taking a breath as if she were about to plunge into a pool, she darted out into the rain. The wind drove the raindrops sideways, drenching her slacks so that they clung to her legs after only a few steps. By the time she neared the car, she was breathless.

Head down, she bolted toward the door and right into the man who waited there.

"Steve." Her breath caught.

He grasped her elbow, supporting her. "I have to talk to you. Please, Caitlyn."

Much as she wanted to hold on to her anger with him, she didn't want to appear childish. And now that she knew what the general was like, she could understand, to some extent, how Steve had gotten into the situation he had.

"Let's get in the car, for goodness' sake." She fumbled with her keys.

In a moment they were both in the front seat. She started the air conditioner to take the moisture out of the air and tried to catch her breath.

"I'm sorry," he said. "You look as if the general gave you a rough time."

She nodded, pushing damp hair out of her face. "I suppose not any worse than he gave you. He does roll over a person, doesn't he?"

"Yes." Steve shook his head, his eyes dark with concern. "I'm sorry I couldn't speak about it before, but now that you've talked to him, it doesn't matter. I told him about Ali's condition and his mother's death. I tried to persuade him to take responsibility for Greg's child, but he wouldn't even consider it. He had disowned Greg a few years ago."

The general's scathing words about his dead son still seemed to ring in her ears. "That's a terrible thing, to cut your own child out of your life."

Steve turned more fully toward her, close in the confines of the small car. "I'm sorry I handled the situation the way I did. If we'd gone together to see him initially, maybe it would have made a difference."

She almost responded sharply that he should have done just that, but she discovered that her anger had slipped away in the past hour.

"To be honest, I don't think it would have made any difference. General Willis has to be the most inflexible person I've ever met."

"The saddest thing is that he doesn't even see that he's hurting himself more than anyone." Steve's forehead creased. "I feel so helpless. I want to minister to him, but he won't let me."

"That really matters to you, doesn't it?" She looked at him, feeling as if she was seeing him in a way she never had before.

Steve cared, really cared deeply, behind that casual, easygoing manner of his. He wanted to love even that brusque, annoying man who was such a roadblock to them.

"Of course." He looked a little surprised, as if any other option hadn't occurred to him.

"You know, people are right about you. You really are a good guy."

He gave her that lopsided smile. "I try. The Lord knows I can't do it on my own."

Usually she would back away from so personal a statement, determined to keep things light and casual. But this was different. They were cut off from the rest of the world with the rain thundering on the car's roof, the fogged windows shutting out everyone and everything but the two of them.

"You depend on your faith."

"I rely on it," he said quietly. "I know that God is always there to help, and that when I try to go it alone, I'll mess up."

She almost envied him for a moment. It would be nice to feel that God cared that much about every detail of your life. "I guess that's where we're different. I've always done everything on my own."

His eyebrow raised. "Everything?"

She shrugged. "It seemed that way to me, anyway. Things weren't so easy for us after Daddy left us. I couldn't put my burdens on Mama—she had enough to deal with. So I learned how to handle things myself."

He reached out to brush a strand of damp hair from her face, his fingers stroking her cheek and setting up a wave of warmth in their wake.

"You were just a kid then," he murmured. "What—ten or eleven?"

"Twelve. Carolyn was only ten, so she needed Mama more than I did."

Concentrate, don't just react to how close he is.

She felt pride in what she'd accomplished, after all. Maybe she'd missed a few things in high school, but she'd done everything on her own, studying harder than anyone, determined that her grades would be the best, that she'd be the one to take home a scholarship, that she'd succeed.

"I don't regret it. It made me strong."

"You were a kid," he said softly. He was so close she could see the fine lines at the corners of his eyes, the white flecks deep in the blue. There was a fine sheen of moisture on his tanned skin.

He leaned closer. She couldn't breathe, couldn't think…

And then his lips found hers, and all she could think about was his embrace.

His lips were warm and firm, and his strong hand cradled her head gently, protectively. Warmth and tenderness flowed through her, and she relaxed into the kiss. The outside world was gone, and she never wanted this moment to end.

Too soon it did. Steve drew back and blinked, seeming to wake himself from the dream they'd momentarily shared.

"I'm not sure I should have done that."

"I'm not either," she said. "But I'm glad you did."

For a moment longer their gazes clung. Then Steve leaned back against the door, as if he needed to put some distance between them.

She cleared her throat.

"What—what are we going to do now?"

His smile flickered. "I did hear you say 'we,' didn't I?"

"We." She nodded slowly, wondering if she was doing the right thing. "Will you work with me on getting Ali here, Steve?"

"I will." His face was solemn, as if he was taking a vow.

Chapter Seven

"Hi, kids." Steve waved to the children playing on the swings in the backyard as he headed into the offices of Children of the Day the morning after his encounter with Caitlyn.

At least the air was clear between them now about the general. He'd been thanking God for that ever since.

Unfortunately, a whole new set of complications had emerged when he'd given in to his longing to hold her in his arms.

Caitlyn had revealed more about herself than she'd probably realized. He'd seen the little girl in her eyes, struggling with making sense of the fact that her father could just walk away from her.

And in the emotion of that moment, he'd just wanted to comfort and hold her. He hadn't thought through the difficulties of getting involved with her.

Caitlyn's life was complicated enough already, dealing with being a mother to the twins, with her own unresolved grief and with the life decisions she had to make.

Adding in a potential relationship, especially with someone here in Prairie Springs, was more trouble she didn't need.

As for him—well, he wasn't sure he was ready for a serious commitment yet. Maybe he never would be.

He should be careful. But he couldn't stay away from Caitlyn, not when a child's life was at stake. So they had no choice but to deal with this.

He tapped on the partially open door to Caitlyn's office, amused that she had adopted Anna's open-door policy already. In response to her voice, he went in, to find her alone and staring at her computer screen. She looked up at his entrance.

"Good morning." Her smile was cool and professional. She had her armor on again, and the vulnerable woman of yesterday was nowhere in sight.

Well, hadn't he just been telling himself that was for the best? He should be pleased.

"Hi." He crossed to the desk and pulled a chair up next to her. "What's happening? Have you found anything yet?"

She handed him a computer printout. "Only bad things, unfortunately. I've had no success with the embassy where Greg Willis would have registered his son's birth."

"They could have left the area for the baby's birth, I guess," he suggested.

Caitlyn leaned back in her chair, frowning. "They could have, but if they did, how are we supposed to find out where? Without some lead, I'm left checking every consulate in the Middle East."

"Not a good option, I agree."

Her frown deepened. "You don't suppose we're on the

wrong track entirely, do you? I mean, we're assuming Ali is Greg's son because of the marriage license, but we don't have a birth certificate to back that up."

That hadn't occurred to him. He stared absently at the list she'd made of avenues they should explore. If Ali wasn't Greg's son—still, if that were the case, wouldn't the general have mentioned it? Of course, he might not know, given the way he'd cut his son off.

"I guess it's possible, but I think we have to go on the assumption that he's Greg's child unless something comes up to disprove it. I had an e-mail from Mike saying he was trying to get in touch with any friends of the mother. That may help."

"Good. What about friends of the father? They might know where the couple was living when Ali was born."

He'd already thought of that. "I've started trying to contact people who served with him. Many of them seem to have left the military since then, so finding them isn't as easy as I'd expected it to be, but I'm sure to catch up with them somehow."

"All right. And I'll keep working on embassies and consulates, as well." Caitlyn was looking at the paper, not at him. "I talked with General Willis's older sister in Austin, who appears to be his only close relative. She can see us this afternoon. Of course, if you're busy, I can go alone."

She almost sounded as if she'd prefer that, but they were in this together.

"No, that's fine with me."

Her eyebrows lifted. "As I've observed before, army chaplains seem to have a lot of freedom."

"We're accountable to a higher authority." He grinned.

"On the other hand, you're accountable to Anna, and she expects results."

"Yes." Her eyes clouded, as if reminded of all that was at stake. "I'd like—"

She cut off abruptly as the door opened again. Jake Hopkins came in, a sheaf of papers in one hand, the other grasping an ebony cane with a silver handle. Jake seemed to enjoy displaying his collection of canes, though he'd immediately shoot down any hint of sympathy for his injury.

"Hey, there, Steve. How you doing, boy?" He nodded to Caitlyn. "When did you hook up with this good ole boy, Caitlyn?"

"Anna wished me on her. It's good to see you, too." He stood to offer a chair to Jake, but Jake shook his head.

"Can't stay long enough to sit."

"You're always in a rush these days—you're startin' to act like a Yankee. You have any good news for us?"

Jake shrugged. "I've told Caitlyn everything I know about the process. I can't do another thing until you come up with a relative and the paperwork we need, so get cracking."

"We are," he protested. "Believe it or not, this is work we're doin' here."

Jake raised an eyebrow in doubt. "Well, I'm on a different errand today." He handed the papers he held to Caitlyn. "These are the forms you need to apply to the Texas bar. I just reckoned I'd drop them off for you."

Caitlyn looked taken aback. "Thanks, but I don't think—"

"Hey, who wouldn't want to practice Texas law?" He turned even as he spoke. "Sorry, I have to go. I'm due in court."

"I thought you were awfully well dressed today." Steve walked to the door with him. "We'll be in touch as soon as we have anything."

"Do that." Jake thumped his way out.

Steve turned back to Caitlyn, eyeing the forms. "So you're thinking of getting licensed in Texas?"

"No." She shoved the forms into a drawer and shut it firmly. "I'm not."

He leaned one hip against the corner of the desk, looking down at her. Didn't she realize yet how much she was needed here?

"Why not? Jake would tell you that Prairie Springs is a pretty nice place to practice law."

Her face seemed to tighten. "I left Prairie Springs to make something of myself. Coming back would be—regressing. I'm not interested in arguing local dog law violations and representing Saturday-night drunks."

"A real type-A high achiever, aren't you? I thought maybe now that you've proved yourself in the big city, you could be happy here. For the sake of your mother and the twins, if not for yourself."

Her hands clenched into fists in her lap. "Maybe they'd all be better off away from constant reminders of their grief."

He wanted to take those strained hands in his, but he didn't dare. "Your grief, too," he said softly. "You never speak of that."

"I'm fine."

"If you keep it locked up inside—"

"Just leave it alone." She glared at him. "You don't have any idea what I'm feeling. Let's get back to business, shall we?"

I do know exactly what you're feeling, Caitlyn. But you wouldn't believe that unless I told you things I have no intention of saying.

"All right," he said. "Sorry. What time shall I pick you up to drive to Austin?"

"Has it occurred to you that a woman who's living in a retirement home might not be eager to take on the responsibility of a five-year-old?"

Caitlyn fretted over Steve's question as he drove his red pickup truck through the scrolled wrought-iron gates of Crestview Estates in Austin that afternoon.

"We don't have too many options." She had to admit, that question had been plaguing her, too. "Maybe she can at least point us in the direction of some more likely relative."

"If there is one." Steve seemed a bit pessimistic for him today.

"Or Miss Willis might be eager to help out. We have to try. At least money probably isn't a deterrent."

"You have a point." Steve leaned forward to peer at a street sign, and she glanced around.

Crestview Estates, with its rolling, manicured lawns, carefully tended flower beds and winding residential streets, was a typical upscale gated community. Whatever facilities there were to extend geriatric care to the residents were well disguised.

"There's the street." She pointed to the sign, half hidden by the arching branches of a cottonwood tree.

During the half-hour drive from Prairie Springs to Austin, they'd kept the conversation strictly on business. She had a sneaking feeling that she needed to apologize for her rudeness that morning, but she didn't want to bring it up.

The truth was that she was afraid of going too deep, of showing too much.

She usually didn't have any trouble keeping things superficial with people. Only Steve seemed to have the ability to force her deeper. With him, she had to have her guard up at all times.

Steve drove down a quiet street lined with elegant homes and pulled into the driveway of a gracious one-story house whose gray shingles blended into the foliage that surrounded it. Everything about the property was immaculate, and it was no doubt cared for by an army of gardeners.

He was already coming around to her door, so Caitlyn opened it quickly and slid out. She preceded him up the three steps to the wide front porch, noting the wheelchair ramp that curved to ground level.

She saw Steve looking at it.

"Maybe all the houses have them."

"Maybe." He was noncommittal.

She rang the bell, and the door was opened immediately by a maid in a neat black uniform. Caitlyn blinked, feeling as if she'd dropped back in time. Who had uniformed maids anymore?

"Ms. Villard and Chaplain Windham to see Miss Willis." She almost felt as if she should have a visiting card to hand over.

"*Sí*, yes, ma'am, she is waiting for you." The smiling young woman closed the door and then led them quickly through an archway into a living room. "They are here, ma'am."

The woman at the window lowered a small pair of binoculars and turned her wheelchair toward them.

"Welcome, both of you. It's nice of you to come all this way." She gestured with the glasses. "I was just watching the birds at the feeder."

Miss Lydia Willis was birdlike herself, tiny and so delicate that it seemed a breeze might blow her off course. She moved the chair closer. Bright blue eyes peered up at them curiously. "You are Ms. Villard?"

"I'm Caitlyn Villard, Miss Willis." She shook hands carefully, half-afraid the woman would bruise. "I'm the care coordinator at Children of the Day in Prairie Springs. And this is Chaplain Steve Windham."

Steve bent over the woman's hand with so courtly an air that it was almost a bow. "A pleasure to meet you, ma'am."

"Please, sit down and tell me how I can help you. You said it had something to do with my late nephew?" Her eyes filled with tears, but she blinked them away.

Caitlyn exchanged glances with Steve. Obviously this fragile elderly lady wasn't going to take charge of a five-year-old. Still, they couldn't know how she might help them unless they tried.

"We've recently learned that Gregory Willis was married while he was deployed in the Middle East," she began. Was this news to the woman? If so, maybe she should have led up to it more gently.

But Miss Willis was already nodding. "Yes, I know about that. Goodness, what a terrible time that was. Marlon, my brother, you know, was absolutely livid about it."

"We know," Steve said, with great understatement.

"You mustn't think Marlon was prejudiced against that

poor young woman because of her background," she said quickly. "I don't believe that was it at all. But Marlon had always envisioned a quick rise to the top in the military for Gregory, and he knew that having married a local person while on deployment would be a terrible obstacle for him."

Steve nodded. "I'm afraid that's true. Like it or not, the army wouldn't consider such a marriage a career asset."

"And I'm sure Marlon thought Gregory was making a mistake, acting out of the emotion of the moment instead of thinking it through properly."

"People in love seldom stop to think things through," Caitlyn said.

Not that she had any personal experience of that. Her romances had always been both brief and rational. She wasn't the type of person to fall head over heels.

"I suppose that's true." Miss Willis wiped her eyes with a lace-edged handkerchief that seemed like a relic of a bygone age. "It was so sad, all of it. Marlon was hasty, acting on impulse himself, saying if Gregory did this he was no son of his. Of course he didn't mean it, but once Marlon said that, he found it impossible to go back on it." She shook her head sadly. "Gregory died, and they'd never made up. Tragic, but at least it's over now."

"Well, not quite." She hated to distress the woman further, but she didn't have a choice. Ali's life hung in the balance. "It's recently come to light that Gregory and his wife had a son. The boy's mother was killed in a bombing, but the little boy, Ali, is safe at an army hospital."

The handkerchief dropped in her lap. "You're sure? Oh my, I can hardly take it in. A little boy. Gregory's son. Does Marlon know?"

"Yes. I talked with him about it," Steve said.

Something in his voice must have alerted her. Her gaze seemed to search Steve's face. "Marlon's being adamant, isn't he? I always said he was the most stubborn man I ever met."

"Yes, ma'am, I'm afraid so. The thing is that it's possible the child may need heart surgery, and we'd like to bring him to the States as soon as possible. But we can only do that if a relative takes legal responsibility for him."

Tears glistened in her eyes again. "Young man, I would do it in an instant. But I don't suppose—" She broke off, gesturing to the wheelchair.

"No, ma'am, I'm afraid the court might not find you well enough to take charge of a young child."

"There must be something I can do." She tapped her fingers on the arm of the chair. "Do you need money?"

"No, we're all right in that respect," Steve said.

"From Marlon, I suppose," she said shrewdly. "He won't bend on his word, but he's not heartless. He wouldn't leave a child in distress."

"Much as we're grateful for the funds," Caitlyn said, "the need for a relative to act as conservator with the court is more pressing. Can you think of anyone, no matter how distant, we might approach?"

The woman shook her head, and Caitlyn's heart clenched. She hadn't realized until this moment how much she'd counted on Miss Willis to come up with something helpful.

"I'm afraid the Willis clan has dwindled to just Marlon and me, without a soul to come after us." She gave a small, ladylike sigh. "To think that Marlon has a grandson, if only he'd get off his high horse and acknowledge the boy."

"He wouldn't listen to us," Steve said. "Do you think you might try to reason with him?"

"I'll try, of course." She sat very erect in the chair. "I can't guarantee he'll listen."

"Anything you could do would help."

Miss Willis nodded. "When I think of how he doted on Gregory, talking about him all the time, showing me endless photos and movies, proud as could be of every accomplishment. It's just not right that he'd turn his back on Gregory's son."

The tears sparkled in her eyes again, and Steve leaned across to put his strong, tanned hand over hers. "Don't distress yourself, Miss Willis. God has a way of working things out, and I have to believe that His eye is on little Ali."

She clasped his hand. "Will you just say a prayer for him with me, Chaplain? I'd like that."

"Of course." Steve reached out to Caitlyn and took her hand, too, holding it in a warm, firm clasp. He bowed his head.

"Father, we know that You care for all Your creations, that not the smallest sparrow falls without Your knowledge. We hold little Ali up to You, asking Your blessing on him. Keep him safe, Father, and show us the way to help him. In Jesus' name, Amen."

"Amen," Miss Willis whispered.

Caitlyn's hand tingled when she drew it away from Steve's clasp. She hadn't seen him in chaplain mode before, and she found her respect for him growing. He did know how to comfort and care, and when he'd prayed, she'd actually prayed with him.

She tried to settle the emotion that seemed to well up

inside her. No matter how much of a good guy Steve Windham was, he wasn't the guy for her, and she'd better remember that.

The chorus of women's voices was so loud when Caitlyn walked into the Fort Bonnell gym on Saturday that she nearly turned around and walked back out again.

How ridiculous was that? If she could walk into a New York courtroom with perfect composure, she could certainly handle a roomful of women packing boxes to send to soldiers.

It was being back in Prairie Springs, she knew that. Here, she felt again like the studious teenage wallflower she'd once been.

Well, she wasn't that person any longer. And she was certainly smart enough to know that most teenagers had feelings of insecurity, even if she hadn't been able to see that then.

She walked along the end of the long rows of tables, searching for someone to tell her what she was supposed to do. Mama had talked her into coming in her place, and since the twins were off on a play date, it had seemed the perfect time to give her mother a break.

The tables were lined primarily with women, although there was a sprinkling of teenagers and a few older men, as well as some men and women in uniform. Everyone seemed to know what to do as they wrapped an assortment of objects to put into the boxes that were headed overseas.

Finally she saw a familiar face. Sarah, the twins' kindergarten teacher, worked at the end of a row. Spotting Caitlyn, she gave her a welcoming smile and gestured her over.

"Your first time?" she asked.

Caitlyn nodded. "I'm taking my mother's place today. I need someone to put me to work."

"Just grab some paper and start wrapping," Sarah said. "And you'd better get used to it. I sometimes find myself wrapping in my sleep. We do this on post once a month, and at Children of the Day once a month, also."

"That's a lot of packages." She pulled out some bubble wrap.

"Nowhere near enough." Sarah's blue eyes darkened with concern. "I'd like to be sure every single soldier got a package from home once a month, but we can't do that. We focus on the units from Fort Bonnell."

Caitlyn, all thumbs at first, got into the swing of things quickly. Items—everything from soap to paperback books to CDs—appeared in front of her, dropped by runners, most of them teenagers who seemed to make a game of it. She and Sarah wrapped and packed until the box was full. Finished boxes were slid under the table to be picked up by another team.

"How are the twins doing?" Sarah seemed to have the routine down pat enough that she could chat without diminishing her speed.

Caitlyn felt her forehead wrinkle and deliberately smoothed it out. "I wish I knew. I guess worrying comes with the territory. Some days I think they're doing well, but then Josie will start having nightmares, or Amanda will get defiant and aggressive, and I wonder if they're making any progress at all."

Sarah's busy hands stilled. "I know how worrisome taking care of kids can be. But it's bound to be up and down. Nothing about children's development goes in a straight line, and that's especially true when they're dealing with grief. This is a huge hurdle for them to overcome."

"Yes." Her throat tightened. "It is."

"It must be so hard for you. You have your own grief to deal with, as well." Sarah's warmth seemed to surround her.

Oddly enough, it was easier to hear that from Sarah than Steve.

"Thanks for your concern." She wrapped a CD with concentrated care. "To tell you the truth, sometimes I just feel so angry with Carolyn. I know that's stupid."

"It's not stupid at all," Sarah said quickly. "Anger is a part of the grieving process." She tilted her head to the side, studying Caitlyn's face. "Have you considered talking to Steve Windham about it? He's very good at counseling the bereaved."

"I—no, I haven't. I mean, we're working together, and maybe it's better not to mix the roles."

"Speaking of Steve, there he is." Sarah nudged her, nodding toward the far end of the room. "He always helps out at these things."

She glanced across the room. Steve, in uniform, bent over a table, talking with one of the volunteers. "He seems to be everywhere."

Sarah chuckled. "I guess he is involved in just about everything that goes on in Prairie Springs. Part of it is his job, I guess, but I think mostly he just has a heart for helping others, especially those who've lost someone. Of course, he really knows how that feels."

Caitlyn blinked, and then turned to look at Sarah. "What do you mean?"

It was Sarah's turn to look surprised. "You didn't know? Well, no, I guess you wouldn't."

"Know what?"

Something bad, obviously. She seemed to feel it looming over her, like a storm about to break.

"Steve was a chaplain with the first wave of invasion troops that went into Iraq. He was engaged then, to another officer. They were going to be married when their deployment was up." Sarah paused. "She was killed in fighting the first month they were there."

It hit her like a blow, and she pressed her palms against the tabletop to steady herself. "I didn't know." Her mouth was so dry she could barely get the words out. "He's never mentioned it."

"He wouldn't." Sarah's voice was weighted with sorrow. "He doesn't talk about it at all."

And she'd rejected his attempts to comfort her, saying he didn't know how she felt. How hurtful that must have been. And how would she face him, knowing it?

Chapter Eight

Caitlyn stood next to her mother as Pastor Fields stretched his arms out in the benediction at the end of the Sunday-morning worship service. His deep voice resounded through the crowded sanctuary.

"Go now in peace, and may the peace of God go with you."

"Amen," the congregation responded in unison, and the organ swelled, filling the high-ceilinged sanctuary with its own Amen.

She wasn't quite sure how she felt about the service this morning. She'd come, as she had since she'd been back in Prairie Springs, because her mother and the twins assumed that she would.

And maybe, if she were truthful with herself, she'd begun to feel the need for spiritual support in the increasingly worrisome effort to save Ali, to say nothing of coping with the twins and helping her mother with her grief.

Pastor Fields had actually been less comforting than challenging this morning, but he certainly had made her think. Caitlyn lingered in the pew as her mother began greeting friends, listening to the organ postlude, her gaze fixed on the stained-glass window of Jesus and his disciples.

Her mind was still caught up in the sermon. Franklin Fields obviously didn't think people were put here to fulfill their own potential, but to do the work God had already prepared for them to do.

Something in her rebelled at that. Wasn't it right to use the talents God had given her? Surely, if she were intended to be doing something else, He wouldn't have given her the drive to succeed as an attorney, would He?

Her internal argument was ended by her mother waving to her from the end of the pew.

"We'd best be getting over to Fellowship Hall, so I can see to my casserole dish."

She nodded, sliding along the pew. There was a potluck lunch after worship today, which apparently happened at least once a month, and her mother had brought what looked like enough food to feed an army.

"Should I go down to fetch the twins?" Amanda and Josie had gone out of the sanctuary after the children's talk, headed for junior church with other children.

Mama shook her head. "Their teacher will bring them up to Fellowship Hall to meet us."

Her mother plowed purposefully through the crowd, intent on her casserole, and Caitlyn followed in her wake, thinking wistfully of Sunday mornings spent with coffee, a bagel, the *Times* crossword and no uncomfortable spiritual challenges.

The vast room that was the center of the church's fellowship was already filling up with people. Several women hustled back and forth between the kitchen and serving tables. Her mother rushed off to join them, and Caitlyn looked around for the twins.

A line of children came through the double doors, breaking apart as kids spotted their families and rushed to join them. Amanda raced across the beige carpeting at full speed and flung herself at Caitlyn's knees, nearly knocking her over.

"I made a boat," she exclaimed, waving her paper craft.

"I did, too," Josie added, coming up behind her a little more slowly. "We had a story about Paul."

"Did you know he was in a wrecked ship?" Amanda said. "That means it had an accident," she added.

"Yes, I think maybe I've heard that story."

Caitlyn knelt to admire the paper boats, complete with a tiny figure meant to be Paul. Josie's was neatly colored, while Amanda had filled in part of a sail and then had apparently become bored and started practicing writing her letters along the hull.

"Here comes Grammy. Maybe we should find seats, and then you can show her your boats."

"Don't worry about sitting down just yet." Her mother came up in time to hear her. "Everyone will visit for a few minutes until Pastor asks the blessing. Now, do be sure you greet all our military guests."

There were quite a few uniforms in the hall, she realized. That must explain why her mother brought so much food.

"Do they all attend worship here?" She'd seen a few uniforms in the sanctuary, but surely not this many.

Mama shook her head. "Most of them worship at Steve's chapel, or one of the other chapels on post. They have a standing invitation to come here for our potlucks, though, and Steve usually rounds up quite a few of them. He's good about that."

Her mother never had anything but praise for Steve. Caitlyn could feel the tension mounting inside her. She'd expected that today, at least, she wouldn't be running into Steve. How on earth would she face him, knowing what she knew now about his loss?

You can never call back a word once it's spoken.

One of the maxims her mother had drilled into her and Carolyn as children surfaced from the recesses of her memory. She should have thought of that before she'd snapped at Steve, rejecting the sympathy he offered.

Steve couldn't know that Sarah had told her about the death of his fiancée. And there was certainly no reason for her to feel disappointment that he hadn't told her himself. They barely knew each other.

And besides, there was that kiss. She might have begun to believe that they were growing closer. But Steve hadn't meant anything by it, obviously. And she shouldn't read anything into it.

"Auntie Caitlyn!" Amanda tugged at her arm, and it sounded as if she'd repeated the name several times. "Guess what?"

"Guess what" was the way Amanda always prefaced something she wanted to be sure you heard and paid proper attention to. "What, Amanda?"

"Some of the kids in Sunday school made cookies and candy and sended it to their soldiers."

"Sent it," she corrected automatically.

"Sent it," Amanda repeated. "Me and Josie want to do that, too."

"We do." Josie grabbed her other arm.

That sounded messy. "But you don't have the names of your soldiers yet."

"Yes, we do," Amanda said. "Mrs. Olga called Grammy and telled her—told her—their names. They're..." She paused, obviously trying to remember.

"Whitney." Josie said the name carefully. "That's the lady. And John. They're married to each other."

"Like Mommy and Daddy," Amanda added.

Her heart squeezed, but she managed a smile. "We'll have to ask Grammy about baking the cookies. It's her kitchen."

Her mother was already nodding. "We'll do it tonight, okay?"

"Aunt Caitlyn, too," Amanda insisted. "She has to help us."

She nodded. "Me, too."

"You too what?" That deep voice from behind her set her heart thudding loudly enough that it resounded in her ears.

"Making cookies, Chaplain Steve." Amanda made a dive for him, grabbing his leg and probably wrinkling his uniform pants. "We're making cookies to send to our soldiers."

"Well, that sounds like a great idea. But are you sure Aunt Caitlyn knows how to make cookies? You might have to teach her." He looked at her, eyes crinkling.

It really wasn't fair for a man to be that attractive. Or to make her heart turn soft at a smile.

Amanda had erupted in giggles. "'Course she does. Everybody knows how to make cookies."

"Not me," he said. "I've never learned. I should have someone like you to teach me."

"Come tonight," Amanda shouted, heedless of her

grandmother's shushing sounds. "Come tonight and help us make cookies."

"Please," Josie added softly, clinging to his hand, her small one lost in his.

His face softened as he looked at Josie.

"If Aunt Caitlyn says it's all right." He looked at Caitlyn, and her heart seemed to melt.

She cleared her throat. "It's fine, if you're sure it's not too much trouble for you to get away from your other duties."

What was she saying? If he came, she'd have to go through several hours with him, trying not to betray the fact that she knew something about him that he'd obviously prefer she didn't.

He smiled, his deep blue eyes taking her breath away. "I wouldn't miss it for anything."

Steve moved Amanda bodily out of reach of the hot oven door as Caitlyn slid a cookie sheet in. Caitlyn closed the door and set the timer.

"Trying to keep from singeing this batch?" he asked, just to tease her. She looked so serious about this whole operation, as if even the cookies she made had to be perfect.

"These aren't burned." She snatched up one of the offending chocolate-chip cookies and took a bite. "Delicious. Just a little bit crispy."

"They're not s'posed to be crispy," Amanda volunteered. "The krispy treats are s'posed to be crispy. Can I have one?"

Caitlyn grabbed her in a big hug and tickled her. "You're going to turn into a cookie if you don't watch out."

Amanda giggled, trying to tickle her back, and the two of them tussled for a moment.

Caitlyn had come a long way from the woman she'd been a few weeks ago. He watched her, smiling a little, as she withstood a tackle from both of her nieces at once.

Then, she'd been so uncomfortable with children that she hadn't even known how to get the twins from the school to the car without a struggle. Now she laughed and hugged easily, showing a warm, loving side that he found very appealing.

And not just with her nieces. He picked up a fork and began flattening the peanut-butter cookies in the crisscross pattern that Amanda had demonstrated. Caitlyn had softened in other ways.

Her determination to solve Ali's problem now seemed motivated as much by her concern for the child as by her need to succeed at every task she undertook. And he'd seen the caring she put into trying to ease Betty's burdens. He could only hope that meant she'd given up any thought of rushing back to the city.

"I want to put more cookies in the tins." Josie climbed on a chair and leaned over the table. "Are these ready, Chaplain Steve?"

He touched the ones she indicated. "They're cool, all right. Pick them up gently, remember."

Josie nodded, bending over the cooling racks, the tip of her tongue sticking out as she concentrated on moving Betty's peanut-butter chocolate-chip oatmeal cookies to the tin.

As usual, Betty had overdone things, insisting on making several different types of cookies as well as the pan of brownies she was frosting at the moment. Still, that batch of oatmeal cookies was probably his fault, since he'd mentioned that they were his favorite.

Amanda went over to her grandmother. "I want to do the frosting," she declared, tugging at Betty's apron. "Please, please, please." Her voice became louder with every word.

He exchanged glances with Caitlyn. *Too much sugar,* she mouthed.

"I love the way you're packing those cookies," he said loudly enough to be heard over Amanda's repeated insistence. "When I was in Iraq a couple of years ago, all the soldiers thought it was the best thing in the world to get a box packed like that."

"It was?" Amanda stopped pestering her grandmother and came to the table. "Why?"

"Why?" He tugged at her ponytail. "Because most of the time we were eating little packages of freeze-dried food." He made a face. "Nowhere near as good as a homemade cookie, believe me. They're the best."

"Who sent you cookies when you were far, far away?" Josie asked.

"My mama did. She sent me all my favorites. And sometimes people from the church would send me a big package. I shared them with all the people who didn't get a package."

"They didn't get any for their very own selves?" Josie's eyes filled with quick tears. "Everyone should get some."

"You're right, sugar." He bent and kissed the top of her head, touched by her compassion. "It can be pretty lonesome when you're deployed. A package makes you feel as if someone loves you."

He remembered, too vividly, what that had been like. For a little while he'd had Elaine, even when they weren't together all the time. But then—

His throat tightened so much that he thought he couldn't speak. Why was it that his grief seemed so near the surface now? Something about what he felt for Caitlyn seemed to have reactivated it, making it harder to keep under control.

He thought, as he often did when he needed guidance, of his father. Daddy had been the exemplar of what a chaplain should be. He'd never have let his own feelings get in the way of what he should do.

"All right, now." Betty turned from the pan of brownies. "That's enough helping for two little girls. It's time to get ready for bed."

That was greeted with groans, of course, but in a few minutes she was ushering them toward the stairs.

"I'll come back and help with the cleanup after I get them to bed," she said.

"No, you will not." Caitlyn put down the spatula she was holding. "You'll go to bed yourself—read, watch TV, knit, if you want to, but do it in bed. You need some rest."

He expected an argument from Betty, but instead she nodded. "I guess I will. Thank you."

Caitlyn watched her mother take the children upstairs, a worried look on her face. "I'm afraid she's still doing too much. I wish—"

"I know." He carried a handful of bowls and spoons to the sink. "But Betty Villard is a hard person to get to slow down. It seems to me you're doing a pretty good job of it."

"I hope so." She carried the rest of the dirty dishes over to the sink. "You don't need to do this. I can take care of it."

Somehow he wasn't ready to leave just yet. "I'll wash.

You dry." He put the stopper in the sink and began running hot water.

She didn't argue either, just grabbed a tea towel from the rack. "I don't think she's sick." She was obviously still talking about her mother. "Just grieving and very tired."

He nodded, realizing that what she needed most now was a listening ear. "You're doing all you can."

"I'm trying." She stared at the bowl she was drying, moving the striped towel around it in slow circles. "I realize there's no chance I'll be able to leave soon. I called a friend of mine, and she's arranging a sublet of my apartment for the next six months."

He was relieved. Surprised, but still relieved. That was what he'd hoped for personally, but this was about her feelings, not his.

"I'm glad you'll have some money coming in from that. What about your job?"

He could feel the tension that gripped her at the question. She was worried about her career—that much was obvious.

"I don't know. At the moment they're holding a place for me. How long they'll be willing to do that, I have no idea." She set the bowl down with a clunk. "I can't lose that position after everything I've sacrificed to get this far. I can't."

She was obviously near tears, and he wasn't sure how to comfort her.

"Talk to me about it, Caitlyn. Why is this particular job so important to you? No one can take your credentials away. There are plenty of other things you can do. You could even go into practice for yourself."

And stay right here for good.

But he couldn't ask her to do anything that implied a future between them. He had to keep this focused on what was best for her, for the twins, for her mother.

She darted him a suspicious look. "You weren't by any chance listening in on Pastor Fields's sermon today, were you?"

"I was too busy giving my own. Why?"

She twisted the tea towel between her hands. "He said that most of the self-improvement models out there get it wrong. He feels that many people put too much emphasis on fulfilling their own potential and not enough on finding the place God prepared for them."

"Sounds like a good sermon."

"Do you agree with that idea?" She impaled him with a look that demanded an honest answer.

"I think that when you're in the place where God wants you, you'll be happy. You'll feel as if you fit." He'd certainly found that to be true in his own life. "Were you happy in your job, or did you do it because—"

He stopped, not sure he should say what he was thinking.

"What? Go on."

He leaned against the sink, watching her. Their faces were very close, and the room very still. "I thought maybe your drive to succeed had something to do with wanting to please your father."

He expected her to flare back at that, but she didn't. She looked up at him, her eyes suddenly wide and lost, all her defiant energy gone.

"It was tough to do that. Carolyn was always his favorite, you know. He laughed and played with her, not with me."

"I'm sure he loved you—" But how could he be sure? He only knew that the man had walked away from his family and never even bothered to support them after that.

She shook her head. "The only time he was pleased with me was when I accomplished something. So I did."

"He was wrong." Criminally wrong, to do that to a child.

"I'm not complaining." She tried to rally. "It gave me the drive to get where I am."

But a tear hung on her lashes, denying the words. He might have been able to hold back, if it weren't for that tear. It cut him right to the heart.

He took her shoulders and drew her into his arms, pressing his cheek against the silk of her hair.

"It's okay," he murmured. "It is, really. He didn't deserve to have a daughter like you." He tilted her face up so that he could see it. "I mean it. You're bright and beautiful and loving and caring—"

His mind stopped working. He bent his head and kissed her.

Her lips softened under his, and she slid her arms around him. It shook him as thoroughly as the kiss they'd shared in the car, but this was better. Her arms were around him and he was holding her close.

What was he doing? He'd already convinced himself that she was off limits. He couldn't be counseling her one minute and kissing her the next, even if he was ready for a relationship. He pulled back. Reluctantly.

"I'm sorry," he whispered. "I shouldn't have."

Her gaze bored into him, as if she'd see to his very soul. "Why not?" Her lips trembled just a little. "That's what you said before. Is it because of your fiancée?"

* * *

Caitlyn froze, appalled at the words that had come out of her mouth.

"I'm sorry—" she began.

Steve shook his head, his face so tight she couldn't read his emotions. He glanced around.

"Let's go outside and get some air."

Not sure she wanted to hear whatever was going to come next, she nodded. He held the door, and they walked out onto the porch that wrapped around the Victorian house.

Dusk had drawn in while they'd been working. The air was still sultry, but a gentle breeze teased at her hair. She crossed to the creaky old porch swing, shifted a patchwork pillow and sat down.

Steve moved as if to sit next to her, then seemed to change his mind and went to lean against the porch railing. "How did you know about her?"

His voice was even, and in the semidark, she couldn't see his expression clearly. Maybe that had been in his mind when he'd suggested they come outside.

"Sarah mentioned it. When we were on post, packing boxes."

He didn't move, didn't speak. And she realized she wanted him to. Despite all her firm assertions that she didn't want to be involved with him, she longed to feel they were close enough that he'd tell her.

"I'm sorry," she said when the silence had stretched on too long. "We weren't gossiping about you. Sarah had forgotten that I wouldn't know, and she made some reference to it. Then she had to tell me."

"It's okay." He sounded more himself now, and the tension inside her eased. "It's no big secret. Everyone here knows."

They know, but they don't talk about it, she realized, remembering Sarah's words.

"What was her name?" She couldn't help but venture the question.

"Elaine." Even in the near dark, she could see how tense his body was. His taut hands pressed against the porch railing. "She was a captain in the unit I accompanied to Iraq."

"I take it you didn't have long together?" she asked gently.

The negative movement of his head was a silhouette. Silence again, and this time she felt she couldn't be the one to break it.

Finally he cleared his throat. "She was killed in action." His tone had a note of finality.

"I'm sorry for your loss." The conventional words had never held so much meaning for her. "And I'm sorry for saying that you didn't understand."

He shrugged. "It's all right." He cleared his throat again. "Even if I hadn't lost someone myself in that way, understanding would still be part of my job."

I don't want to be part of your job, Steve. Don't you get that?

She tried to tell herself that it didn't matter, that she wasn't disappointed.

But that would be a lie. She couldn't kid herself about this any longer.

She'd tried not to care, but it had slipped up on her when she wasn't looking. Ironic, wasn't it? She was finally ready to open her heart, and she'd picked a man whose own heart was securely shut.

Chapter Nine

Steve slid a hymnal into the rack and glanced around the small sanctuary of the Fort Bonnell Christian Chapel. Everything was ready for the next service. He had a couple of volunteers to do the actual cleaning up, but still, he always wanted to check things out for himself.

There were times, even after two years here, that he still felt like an impostor when he stood in front of the congregation. His father had been such a commanding presence when he spoke from that same pulpit.

In spite of the personnel turnover that was natural on any army post, people still mentioned his daddy and asked how he and Mama were doing. It was good to think he'd had such an influence on people.

Maybe he should talk with his father about this situation with General Willis. Ask for his advice. But he was somehow reluctant to do that. He ought to be able to minister to the general himself, if that was what God willed.

He sank down on the front pew, his gaze fixed on the simple gold cross placed on the plain cream wall in front of him. Everything about the chapel was simple, and that was fine with him. That was what a military chapel should be.

After spending time in a war zone giving sermons perched on the back of a tank, he found he didn't need stained glass or padded pews to keep his attention focused on worship. Brushing that close to death every day had been great training in mental discipline.

Now he'd sought out the quiet of the chapel because he was troubled, and not just about Ali and General Willis.

He bowed his head. *Lord, I don't know what to do with these feelings for Caitlyn. Each time I'm with her I seem to care a little more, but those very feelings seem to make me think about Elaine. Please, guide me to do the right thing.*

He leaned back, rubbing the nape of his neck as he stared at the cross. He'd been avoiding the obvious answer, and maybe he'd better face it.

Possibly the only reason God had brought Caitlyn into his life was so that he could help her become a mother to those two little girls. Their time together might have nothing to do with him, and everything to do with those precious children.

If so, that should be enough for him.

Guide me, he murmured again, and rose. He should check with his secretary and see if the call he was expecting had come through.

As he approached it, the door leading to the hallway and his office swung open. Caitlyn came in, blinking for a moment at the sunlight that poured through the plain glass of the windows.

"Caitlyn." It startled him, having her so close. "What brings you here?"

Your relationship is nothing more than platonic. He reminded himself. *So stop noticing how the breeze had teased tendrils of her golden-brown hair in her face, and how the green of her shirt brought out the greenish tones of her hazel eyes.*

She looked a little surprised. "You called me, remember? Anna left your message on my desk."

"You didn't need to make a special trip." He gestured to the pew, and when she sat down, he sat next to her. But not too close.

"I had to come on post anyway, to pick up some things that are being donated for the Children of the Day fund-raiser. Have you learned anything new about Greg Willis?"

"Not yet, but it's looking hopeful. I finally found someone who served with Greg at about the right time."

"What did he say?" Caitlyn's face lit with hope.

"I haven't spoken with him yet, but I talked with his wife. She said she'd have him call me as soon as he came in." He glanced at his watch. "Which should be soon."

"Thank goodness." Caitlyn's words were heartfelt. "I was beginning to feel as if every effort we made was doomed to failure. If this man knew Greg at the right time, surely he'll know where Ali was born."

"Paul Peterson. They were in the same outfit, and my sources said they were close friends. He's retired from the service, so it took a little time to track him down."

He looked at his watch again, willing the man to call.

Lord, we need a break if we're going to succeed. Please, let this man lead us to some answers.

Caitlyn glanced around the sanctuary, with its rows of

blond wood benches and its simple windows. "So this is your chapel."

"Not really mine." He smiled. "Before you came in, I was thinking that sometimes I feel as if my daddy's still in charge here."

To his surprise, she didn't smile in return. "I'd think that might make your job a little difficult. Feeling as if you're following in his footsteps, I mean."

He considered. "He *is* a tough act to follow, in a way. He was absolutely dedicated to his calling. That was one thing my brother and I learned early as kids—that Daddy's chaplaincy wasn't just a job, and that it had to come first."

She tilted her head to the side, that silky hair caressing her shoulder. "That seems a little hard on his family."

"Don't get me wrong," he said quickly. "He's the greatest. If I can be half the chaplain he was, I'll be happy."

"It must be nice to feel that way about your father." Now it was Caitlyn whose gaze was fixed on the cross, as if she looked for answers there.

He leaned his elbow on the back of the pew, so that he could face her more fully. He wanted to see her face. "Do you ever hear from him?"

"I get a Christmas card from time to time. And sometimes a check for my birthday, although often as not, it would arrive on Carolyn's birthday instead of mine."

"That's rough."

Her face clouded a little. "Carolyn's birthday is next week, did you know that? I'm not sure how to deal with that with the girls."

"Have they mentioned it to you?"

"Not yet. Dates don't mean much at their age. I don't

know whether I should just ignore it and hope they don't remember, or bring it up and see how they feel."

He didn't have an answer for this one. "Maybe you should talk to Olga about it. She's the expert, especially with children, and they may have mentioned it to her."

"That's true." She shook her head. "It's silly, I suppose, but I keep thinking I should know these things by instinct."

That one he did know that answer to. "Even birth parents struggle with issues like that. You're not alone in needing help."

Her lips curved slightly. "You're really good at making people feel better, you know that?"

That smile had his gaze riveted to her face. So maybe it was a good thing that the door swung open again. Joannie Parker, his secretary, came in holding the cordless phone aloft.

"It's that call you were expecting." She glanced from him to Caitlyn, her eyes bright with curiosity as she handed him the phone.

"Thanks, Joannie." His heart thudded. *Please, let this be the lead we've been looking for.*

"I'll leave you alone," she said, and went back through the door toward the office.

He pressed the phone to his ear, very aware of Caitlyn's gaze on his face. She was depending on this so much. He just hoped she wasn't going to be disappointed.

"Thanks so much for calling back, Mr. Peterson. I wanted to talk with you about an army buddy of yours, Gregory Willis."

A few minutes later, he knew neither one of them would

be disappointed this time. He had to struggle to control his grin as he expressed his thanks and hung up.

Then he looked at Caitlyn, the smile splitting his face. "He knew! Greg took his wife to Athens for the baby's birth. It seems she had a friend who was a doctor there. So if Greg followed the rules, that's where he'd have registered the baby's birth—at the American embassy in Athens."

"What a relief!" She grabbed his arm, holding it tight in her excitement. "That's the first break to come our way. Steve, we may actually be able to do this!"

Her face was lit with happiness, and her eyes danced as she looked up at him. It took everything he had to keep his emotions in control.

He had to. Because otherwise he might have been tempted to kiss her again, and that was exactly the wrong thing to do.

No reply yet from the embassy in Athens.

Caitlyn swung away from the computer in the family room that evening. She hadn't quite figured out the time difference between Texas and Greece, but people did e-mail at any time of the day or night. The answer could come through at any moment.

She stood, stretching. By the time she had gotten the twins to bed, all she wanted to do was collapse in a chair. How her mother had managed to take care of them all these months, she couldn't imagine.

"All finished?" Mama, sitting at the kitchen table with a glass of sweet iced tea, smiled at her.

Caitlyn nodded, crossing the family room to join her. She stepped on something, discovered a marker one of the twins had missed during cleanup and put it on the breakfast bar that separated the two rooms.

"The message I hoped for hasn't come through yet, but I guess it's still early for an answer."

Mama, who'd heard about little Ali and his problems, nodded understandingly. "Surely you'll hear something soon. I'll keep praying."

"Thanks, Mama."

She poured a glass of tea from the pitcher on the counter, added ice and sat down across from her mother, wondering how to bring up the subject that had been needling her for the past few days.

"There was an e-mail from Whitney for the girls," she said. That was the first thing her eyes had been drawn to when her e-mail appeared, even before work. "They'll want to hear it first thing in the morning."

"That's so nice. She really seems to be enjoying writing to the children as much as they like writing to her." Her mother turned the cold glass on the tabletop, making a small ring of condensation. "I confess, I had my doubts about this at first, but it seems to be working out all right."

Caitlyn nodded. "It's so strange, reading about Whitney's life there. I'd be terrified, but she just seems so upbeat."

"That's how Carolyn was." Her mother's voice was soft. "I'm sure she must have been worried and missing the children terribly, but she always sounded positive when she wrote and called."

Caitlyn wanted to say that Carolyn should never have gone, but she bit back the words. It would only upset Mama, and no words could change things now.

Maybe the only way to ask the one question gnawing at her was to blurt it out. She took a breath. "Do you know why Carolyn and Dean picked me to be the twins' guardian?"

Her mother looked startled. "Well, who else would they choose?"

"You. One of their married friends. I know Dean didn't have any family, but surely—"

Her mother's face clouded. "Are you saying you don't want to be the children's guardian?"

"No, no, that's not it at all." She clasped her mother's hand warmly. That was why she'd hesitated to ask the question. She'd been afraid Mama would misunderstand. "It's just that Carolyn and I weren't, well, very close." That was the understatement of the year, wasn't it? "And she never even talked to me about it."

"She should have." Mama's hand clasped hers. "I told her that, but she kept putting it off."

That was Carolyn's nature, of course. She'd always put off the things she didn't want to do, leading to countless Sunday nights staying up late, trying to get her homework finished before school on Monday. But this was considerably more serious.

"The letters from Whitney have made me think more about Carolyn," she said. "About the decisions she had to make when she knew she was going to be deployed."

Mama nodded. "It was a difficult time."

"I guess I just wanted to know what was in her mind when she made the decision. Did she pick me because I was the only person available?"

"Oh, darlin', no!" Her mother's eyes darkened with emotion. "Goodness, that wasn't her thinking at all. We did talk about it a bit. She and Dean both realized that at my age, raising those two girls wasn't a good idea."

She wasn't sure the short term had been a good idea, either, but she knew better than to bring that up.

"Carolyn named you as guardian because she admired you," Mama said. "I suppose she never told you that, but she always bragged about her big sister—how smart and efficient and successful you are. When it came right down to it, she knew she could count on you to do the very best for her children."

There was a lump in her throat that threatened to choke her. "I never knew. We were always so different. It seemed we had nothing in common."

"When you were children—" Her mother stopped, as if she had difficulty speaking, as well. "I think that your father may have contributed to the differences between you two." She shook her head. "Well, that's past history, isn't it?"

Was it? Was it really in the past if it affected what she did and how she felt today?

Mama patted her hand. "I just wish you two could have spent more time together as adults. I think you would have learned to be friends."

Friends. She felt her heart twisting at her mother's words. "I wish that, too," she whispered. "I do."

She'd do her best, Caitlyn thought as she watched the twins in the swimming pool the next afternoon. In the light of day, she wasn't positive her mother had been right about Carolyn's motivation, and she wasn't sure she'd entirely forgiven her sister for the choices she'd made, but that didn't seem to matter so much.

The children were what was important. Carolyn had entrusted them to her.

The swimming lesson was over, and the twins were playing with their friends in the shallow end of the pool. Smiling, she watched Amanda make a valiant effort to swim on her back and go bubbling under, to come up spitting water.

The truth was, she loved those children, and she'd find a way to do her best for them.

Someone stopped next to her, and she looked up to see Steve, in swim trunks, with a towel slung over his shoulder.

"Aren't you going in today?" He lifted one eyebrow in a question.

"I'm not much of a swimmer." While Carolyn had spent summers at the pool, she'd been working, saving money for college. "You enjoy it."

"Will do."

His smile was as friendly as always, but somehow she felt that he was keeping his distance. Having regrets about how close they'd gotten? Probably so.

She watched as he dived into the deep end, his movements sure and confident. He swam underwater for the width of the pool and backstroked across, his strokes even, eating up the distance easily. He held on to the side for a moment, seeming to watch the children playing, and then swam toward the shallow end, submerging when he reached the rope.

He surfaced next to Amanda, making her squeal, and in another moment all the children had joined her in an effort to dunk him.

Steve had a nice way with children, always seeming to

know who needed to be drawn into things, who needed a firm hand. Even as she thought that, he shook his head at Amanda, who was splashing her sister. The little girl desisted, far faster than she would have for Caitlyn.

She was drifting, Caitlyn realized. Not just at the moment, sitting in the sun half-asleep, but in making decisions about her future.

Why does it have to be so hard? It no longer seemed so unfamiliar to pray. In fact, it was becoming a larger and larger part of her internal conversations.

Lord, I just don't understand. I'm trying to do my best for the children, but does that mean I have to give up the career that means so much to me? I do good work there, don't I?

She could practice law in Texas, of course, but that wasn't her dream. It wasn't what she'd worked so hard for all these years. Did she have to surrender that?

If she asked Steve that question, he'd have an answer. He thought he knew what she ought to do, and he never seemed hesitate to tell her. Which was an awfully good reason not to ask him.

Some of the mothers were gathering up beach towels and calling their children out of the pool. She glanced at her watch. It was about time to head home. Steve came toward her, wading through the water, the twins hanging on to his hands.

"Get wet, Auntie Caitlyn." Holding the edge of the pool, Amanda splashed her, and the water felt beautifully cool on her legs.

"No, thanks." She drew her legs back. "You were doing a great job in your lesson. You, too, Josie. I liked the way you floated on your back."

"I'm going to swim well enough to go in the deep end pretty soon," Amanda said, pulling herself out of the pool and standing dripping until Caitlyn wrapped a towel around her. "And when I can swim in the deep end, I'll go off the high dive, just like Mommy used to."

She was mentioning her mother more easily in conversation these days, and that had to be good, didn't it?

"Your mommy was a good swimmer."

"And diver," Josie said. "I 'memer when she went off the high dive. I want to do it, too."

"You're a scaredy-cat," Amanda said. "You won't do it."

"Will too," Josie said predictably, her lower lip trembling.

"Neither of you will do it until you can swim much, much better than you can right now," Caitlyn said firmly. "And I won't do it at all."

"You won't?" Amanda stared at her, surprised, maybe even a little disappointed. "Why not?"

It hadn't occurred to her that it would be hard to admit she couldn't do something to a child, but it was.

"I'm not a very good swimmer," she said. "And I was always afraid of the high dive."

Carolyn had teased her to go up one day, she remembered. Her annoyance with Carolyn for embarrassing her in front of their friends had been enough to get her partway up the ladder. And then she'd panicked and scrambled back down again.

"You're afraid." Amanda looked at her as accusingly as if she'd committed a sin.

Before she could think of an answer to that, Steve spoke.

"Everyone's afraid of something," he said. "It's unkind to tease them about it. You wouldn't want them to tease you about the things you're afraid of."

"They couldn't," Amanda declared. "'Cause I'm not afraid of anything."

"Not anything?" Steve asked gently. "Not loud thunderstorms or the dark?"

Amanda blinked. "Well, maybe the dark. Just a little bit."

"Me, too." Josie came to Caitlyn for her towel. "And I don't like loud thunder or big dogs."

Caitlyn wrapped the towel around her, holding Josie close when she shivered.

"What are you scared of, Chaplain Steve?" Amanda sounded determined to get an admission out of him.

He bent over her. "You really want to know?" he asked.

She nodded.

"Nosy little girls," he declared, and tickled her.

What are you afraid of, Chaplain Steve? She wouldn't ask, but she wanted to know. *Does it have anything to do with your lost love?*

Chapter Ten

"Chaplain Steve, Chaplain Steve!"

Steve lifted the stack of boxes he carried just as Amanda and Josie barreled into his legs. That seemed to be the twins' standard form of greeting, but he hadn't expected to run into them at the elementary-school gym this afternoon.

"Hi, gang. Take it easy, okay? I'll get into trouble if I drop these boxes."

He juggled the boxes into one arm so he could ruffle the twins' chestnut hair. They wore identical denim shorts and striped blue-and-white shirts today, but he could always tell them apart.

"What's in them?" Amanda scrutinized the cardboard cartons, as if assessing the likelihood that they contained toys.

"Prizes for the games at the carnival. Do you think you'll win one?"

"I will, I will." Amanda bounced up and down. "Grammy says I can play the fish game and the throwing-the-ball game, and maybe even get some cotton candy, 'cause all the money is for poor children."

"That's right." He hefted the boxes. "That's why lots of people are donating prizes, too. Because all the money we raise at the carnival will help children."

Betty hurried up to him, looking distracted. "Are those prizes? They go right on that table." She gave Amanda a gentle push. "Stay out of Chaplain Steve's way, please, girls. Everyone has work to do."

"They're fine," Steve said quickly. "In fact, maybe between them, they could carry one of these boxes for me. Do you two think you're strong enough?"

"I can do it," Amanda exclaimed, and Josie nodded solemnly.

Steve bent to let them take the lightest carton off the top of the stack. They balanced it between them, hanging on with both hands, and followed as their grandmother led the way to the table where the boxes of prizes were stacked.

Steve smiled at the identical expressions on their intent little faces. He ministered to every bereaved person in the Fort Bonnell family, but he'd have to admit that the twins had a special place in his heart.

The table was filling up with cartons containing all sorts of prizes, and he was sure there'd be more coming in. Everyone rallied around when it came to raising money for Children of the Day, Prairie Springs's favorite charity.

Funny, how even people who'd been doubtful at first about Anna's grand idea, now bragged that the foundation was known around the world for its good work.

"Caitlyn's not around today?" He posed the question casually once the boxes were put away.

"She'll probably pop in soon. She said she had some work to do at the office before she came." Betty pushed up her glasses, put her hands on her hips and looked around the gym. "Goodness, do you think we'll ever be ready in time?"

All around them, half-finished booths fought for space with half-erected games. Two volunteers were attempting to hang a banner that read, Children of the Day Charity Carnival across the width of the gym, and a makeshift stage at one end of the long gymnasium was still just a pile of lumber.

"It'll be fine," he said. "It looked terrible at this point last year, but we managed to have everything ready on time, remember?"

Behind her glasses, Betty's eyes glistened, and he realized that last year, Carolyn had been one of their most faithful volunteers.

She cleared her throat. "Yes, I guess you're right about that."

"Steve, how about getting us some more volunteers?" Anna said, pausing as she passed, like a hummingbird in flight. "We need more muscle to get these booths finished. Can you bring us some military?"

"Yes, ma'am." He saluted. "I'll get on that right away."

Anna grinned. "Sorry. I didn't mean to be bossy. I'm a little distracted. Oh, there's Sarah. I have to talk to her about the balloons." She rushed off.

"Look. There's your teacher, Ms. Sarah." He pointed her out to the twins. "Why don't you go say hi."

Betty looked as if she could stand a moment's break to regain her composure.

"We'll tell her we're going to be in her class, just in case she forgot," Amanda said. Grabbing Josie's hand, she scurried off.

"Are you okay?" He bent over Betty, wishing he could take back his casual words.

"I'm fine." She patted his arm. "It's nothing you said, dear. Really. You get on with your work."

He nodded. "Well, I'd better bring another load in from the truck before Anna comes back and catches me loafing." But when he turned toward the door, Caitlyn was entering.

She glanced around the room, spotted him with her mother and came rushing over. Her eyes danced with excitement. Something must have happened.

"Hi, Mama. Steve, you're just the person I wanted to see. Guess what?"

"You sound like Amanda," he teased. "I'm guessing it's something good."

Distracted, she glanced around. "Where are the children?"

"Over there with Sarah," her mother said. "I'm just going to run to the kitchen and check the coffee while they're occupied." Betty hurried off on her self-appointed rounds.

He caught Caitlyn's hand and just as quickly dropped it. The power of her touch was just too strong.

"Come on, tell me," he said.

She blinked, as if recalling her attention. "I have it! The embassy sent us confirmation of Ali's birth registration and a copy of the birth certificate. We've done it, Steve."

"Praise God. That's terrific." He didn't need to be touching her, he realized, to feel that pull. "We're getting there."

"We are." But she sobered. "I have Jake working on a plan of action if we can't get the general on board. It won't be easy. Have you heard anything at all from Miss Willis?"

"I talked with her about it this morning. She said not to

count on his support yet, but that she's been working on him. I guess all we can do is pray she succeeds."

"I have been," Caitlyn said softly.

"So have—"

He cut off what he was saying at the sound of a cry, but he wasn't as fast as Caitlyn, who had already left his side.

He swung around, a wordless prayer forming in his mind, and spotted the source immediately.

Amanda clung to a board, halfway up the unfinished stage. She stared down, openmouthed, at Josie, lying crumpled underneath.

"How much farther?"

Caitlyn sat in the backseat of her car, holding a compress against the cut on Josie's forehead, while Steve drove them to the emergency room. Josie leaned close against her, whimpering a little.

"We're almost there. Hold on, sweetheart." His gaze met Caitlyn's in the rearview mirror. "You hold on, too," he said. "I know the injury looks scary, but I don't think it's too bad."

She tried to manage a smile, without much success. "Sarah said she didn't think it would even need stitches. And I'm sure she's seen plenty of children's bumps and cuts."

She was repeating the kindergarten teacher's words to reassure herself as much as anything.

In that instant when she'd heard the cry, she'd known it was Josie without even looking. Maybe she was actually developing some maternal instincts.

"I should never have taken my eyes off them."

"Don't start blaming yourself." Steve's tone was brisk.

"Every parent feels that way when a child is hurt, but you can't wrap them in cotton at this stage. Five is old enough to trust with a bit of independence."

"I'm sorry," Josie wailed suddenly. "I'm sorry. I didn't mean to be naughty."

"Sweetheart, I know that. It's all right. I'm not mad at you." She kissed Josie's cheek gently.

She and Steve both knew who had instigated climbing on the makeshift stage. Amanda had led, and Josie had followed, of course.

"The doctor is going to fix your forehead up as good as new, I promise."

"I don't want a doctor. I want to go home."

"Hush now. You have to let the doctor take a look at it, so we'll know how to take care of you. Then we'll go home, and you can tell Grammy and Amanda all about the hospital."

They'd convinced her mother that it would be best if she took Amanda home while Caitlyn and Steve went to the hospital. Mama had been so upset—blaming herself, of course.

Still, Steve was right. Both of the girls had known they were doing something they shouldn't.

At some point it would be appropriate to point out to Josie that she didn't have to do everything Amanda did. But that time wasn't now.

"Here we are." Steve pulled up to the E.R. entrance, stopped and turned the blinkers on. He slid out and hurried around, coming to the backdoor and opening it.

"I can take her," she said, but Steve was already lifting Josie out.

"I'll carry her in and then come back to move the car."

Caitlyn nodded and followed him inside, her prayers flowing quickly.

Despite her fears, the emergency room ran smoothly and efficiently. By the time Caitlyn had filled out the paperwork, the nurses were ready to take Josie back to an exam room.

There things slowed down, however. Josie looked forlorn and tearful, lying on the high white table, and nothing Caitlyn could think of to say seemed to cheer her up. The door swung open finally, but it was Steve, not the promised doctor.

"How are we doing?" He sent an inquiring glance toward her while he bent over to give Josie a quick kiss, and she was suddenly, irrationally, glad that he was there to help.

"We're waiting for the doctor."

"I don't want a doctor," Josie wailed. "Manda said he'll sew me up with a big needle."

"Amanda doesn't know anything about it. She's never even been to an emergency room." Caitlyn smoothed the bangs back from the little girl's forehead. "Remember, you're going to tell her all about it when we get home."

"You'll be the one who knows about it," Steve pointed out. "Not Amanda."

"Oh." Josie seemed to absorb that. "I still don't want to get sewed."

"Well, let's have a look and see what's what," the doctor said, coming in. She was a brisk young woman with a warm smile. "What have you been doing with yourself, young lady?"

"I climbed up 'cause Manda said to." Josie pouted. "I'm not going to do that anymore."

"Manda is her twin," Caitlyn explained.

"You have a twin sister?" The doctor checked her over with gentle, efficient movements while she talked. "That must be fun. Can people tell you apart?"

"Mostly," Josie said. She seemed to be losing her fear under the doctor's friendly manner. "Sometimes somebody might call me Manda if they don't know us very much, but I just tell them I'm Josie."

"Good for you." The doctor looked up at Caitlyn. "I don't think we need stitches. We'll just clean up the cut and put a butterfly on it."

"A butterfly?" Josie's eyes went wide.

"Not a real one, sugar." Steve leaned over, holding her hand. "That's a kind of bandage."

"A special one," the doctor said, nodding to the nurse who'd followed her in with a tray. "Now, if Mommy will just hold her head still on this side, we'll get that all cleaned up."

Caitlyn took Josie's head in her hands where the doctor indicated, not bothering to correct the assumption. She was grateful there would be no stitches. She didn't think she could watch that.

Surprisingly, Josie didn't cry during the cleaning. Her eyes filled up at one point, but she clutched Steve's hand tightly and kept her gaze fixed firmly on Caitlyn's face.

Caitlyn murmured softly to her, the kind of soothing nonsense she remembered Mama saying when she'd hurt herself as a child. It seemed to work.

Finally the bandage was on. The doctor smiled at them.

"All finished. Trust me, it's always harder on the parents than on the child. The nurse will give you an instruction sheet, and you can check with her pediatrician in a day or two if you want."

"Thank you."

They weren't the parents, she and Steve. But for a moment, she felt as if they were.

Caitlyn had to force her feet to keep moving after she'd tucked in both the girls and her mother. Mama had been wiped out by the emergency, and she hadn't objected to having an early night. And Amanda had been too intimidated by the havoc she'd caused to put up any bedtime arguments.

Caitlyn felt ready to collapse, herself, but Steve had insisted on coming back to see if they needed anything, and he was still in the family room.

She'd been so thankful for his help. Just having another person Josie loved and trusted there had made all the difference.

But she shouldn't lean on him. It wasn't fair to either of them.

She found Steve on the sofa in the family room, paging through a photo album. She caught a glimpse of the pictures and tensed up.

"Where did you get that?"

He looked up, obviously surprised at her tone. "It was right here, on the coffee table. Is something wrong?"

"Sorry." She sank onto the sofa, pushing her hair back from her face with a sigh. "I didn't mean to snap. I guess Mama was looking at it."

"Problem?" He waited for more.

"It's just that she gets out the photo albums and looks at Carolyn's pictures when she's feeling low. I think the approach of Carolyn's birthday is hurting her more than she wants to let on."

"The first year is always hard." Steve's eyes seemed to turn a deeper shade of blue with empathy. "There are all those holidays to get through for the first time without the person you love."

"I guess so." Steve certainly had more experience in dealing with this sort of thing than she did. "But getting out the albums, crying over the pictures—wouldn't it be better if she didn't dwell on her loss so much?"

"She's always thinking about Carolyn, you know, even when she doesn't talk about her. Maybe she's taking comfort from looking at the photos of happier times, even if it makes her cry."

She leaned back against the cushions, her gaze on his strong face. "Does that work for you?"

His hand clenched on the album. "This isn't about me. I'm here to help you."

Frustration rose in her, and she shook her head. He was so good at evading anything personal. "I wanted to talk with you as a friend, not as a pastor."

For a moment he didn't speak, and she wondered what he was thinking. "I guess I can't really separate them," he said finally. "Maybe it would be better if I could, but I can't."

"Is that something they teach you in seminary?"

"Not exactly. I probably absorbed it a long time ago, from my father. He believed a pastor always had to be strong for the people who depended on him."

She considered that. "Don't you think people might be helped by seeing that you have problems, too? Seeing how you deal with personal hurts?"

He didn't answer, but a muscle twitched in his jaw.

"Sorry." Obviously she couldn't change him. "I didn't

mean to bug you about it. Let me see what you were looking at."

"Early high-school years, I think." He seemed relieved at the change of subject. He handed over the album. "Carolyn with a bunch of giggling girls, all hanging on the fence at a football game."

"Carolyn's posse, we called them." She stared at the young faces, wondering where they all were now. "You know, I used to envy Carolyn in a way. She made friends so easily. She just had to laugh, and people were drawn to her."

"And you?" He propped his arm on the back of the couch, facing her.

She shrugged. "You know who I was in the high-school pecking order. The brain, the geek, the wallflower—whatever you want to call it."

"I wouldn't have described you that way. You just always seemed too preoccupied with making all A's to be bothered with the kind of petty things that interested most of us."

She flipped a page. Carolyn, again surrounded by friends, on the pep squad, waving pompoms in the air. Did Steve really think she hadn't minded being the one who was always on the outside?

"I told myself that I wasn't interested in the frivolous stuff that Carolyn was into. I was too busy getting ready to take the world by storm. But maybe at some level, I wanted to be like her."

She touched the image of Carolyn's smiling face, and her throat clogged with tears. "She was so young." The tears spilled over, and she wiped them away quickly. "Sorry," she muttered. "I don't know what's wrong with me. I never cry."

"It's been an emotional day," he said, his voice low and soft. "You're allowed."

Her control, always so solid, seemed to shimmer. To shatter. "I let Carolyn down." She put her hands to her face. "I let Josie get hurt."

"Oh, Caitlyn, don't." His voice sounded affected by tears as well. "Don't, sugar. It wasn't your fault. It wasn't."

His arm slid around her, and she buried her face in his shoulder, letting herself absorb his warmth and comfort.

She shouldn't. She shouldn't depend on him. But right now, she couldn't seem to help it.

Chapter Eleven

Steve had been right about one thing, Caitlyn decided the next day as she turned onto a quiet residential street in Prairie Springs. She was affected more than she'd realized by her memories of Carolyn.

She'd known, intellectually, that grieving took time, but she hadn't understood at the deepest level just how difficult it would be. The longer she was here, around her mother and the twins, the more acute her grief seemed to become.

The answer was, as it always had been for her, to keep busy. That had gotten her through every other crisis in her life, including her father's desertion, and it would get her through this.

She'd been invited to lunch with Sarah Alpert today, and later she'd be totally preoccupied with the charity carnival. That would keep her too busy to think. In a few more days Carolyn's birthday would be in the past, and they would all start to feel better.

She drew up at the number Sarah had given her, only to realize that Sarah Alpert's small yellow craftsman bungalow was directly across the street from General Willis's imposing residence. She should have noticed the similarity of the addresses, but she hadn't been thinking about that.

She eyed the general's place cautiously, but no one was visible out on the lawn or at the windows. She slid out of the car, forced herself not to look over her shoulder at the house and hurried to Sarah's door, feeling as if the general might emerge at any moment and order her off his street.

"Caitlyn, welcome." Sarah opened the door before she could knock, her smile warm.

Everything about Sarah was warm, she decided, from the firelight glow of her red hair to the caring expression in her eyes. The only surprising thing was that she poured all that warmth and caring onto other people's children, instead of onto a family of her own.

"I didn't know you lived across from—" She stopped, realizing too late that she couldn't explain how she knew the general.

Sarah glanced at the place across the street before ushering Caitlyn in and closing the door.

"Don't worry about it," she said. "You didn't give anything away. I already know that General Willis is Ali's grandfather."

Caitlyn blinked. "You know? But how did you find out? I haven't said anything to anyone but Anna and Steve. General Willis doesn't want it known, I'm afraid, which is making everything so difficult."

"I realize that." Sarah brushed a strand of long red hair back over the shoulder of the simple white T-shirt she wore with cutoffs. "But I was helping Anna with some of the medical paperwork on Ali, and she let it slip. I won't say anything about it to anyone."

"Thanks." Caitlyn smiled ruefully. "The man scares me to death, to be honest. I don't want him thinking I told his secret."

"Marlon Willis isn't a bad guy, although he can seem pretty crusty. He's just unforgiving about his son, I'm afraid."

Sarah led the way through a living room filled with chintzes and plants and into a dining nook that overlooked a tiny back garden that was as charming as the house.

"Yes, he is." Caitlyn thought of his harsh words. "I have trouble understanding how he can still carry a grudge against Gregory years after his death. Or how he can refuse to recognize his only grandchild."

"Please, sit down." Sarah nodded to one of the two chairs that were drawn up to the drop-leaf table. "Would you rather have iced tea or soda?"

"Tea, please, Sarah. This is lovely. You have a charming house."

She went into the adjoining kitchen. "Thanks. I was lucky to find something I could afford in the historic district. I love living here."

Caitlyn heard the clinking of ice cubes in the kitchen. In a moment Sarah returned with a pitcher and two frosted glasses.

"You know, as far as General Willis is concerned, I don't see how he imagines he can keep this a secret." Sarah poured tea into one of the glasses and topped it with a sprig of mint. "Once Ali gets here, whether he claims the boy or not, word is going to get out. He's naive to think anything else."

Caitlyn stared at her for a moment. "You know, that's true. Steve and I have been looking at his refusal to accept the boy from such a narrow angle that we never thought of that."

"Maybe the general didn't, either." Sarah frowned. "I'd hate to think of him taking Ali just because of public opinion, though. That poor child needs to have someone who will love him."

Sarah said the words with such passion that Caitlyn's throat tightened. Here was someone who really cared. "You sound as if you'd like to mother him."

"I'd like to mother all of them. There are way too many lonely, hurting children in the world." Sarah shook her head, as if reminding herself that was impossible. "Goodness, I'm forgetting myself. Let me get the salads. I hope the tea isn't too strong."

"Wonderful." She took a sip of the sweet tea that was fragrant with mint. "This is so nice of you."

"I've wanted a chance to get to know you a little better." Sarah came back with plates bearing flaky croissants piled high with chicken salad. She slid into her seat. "Do you mind if I ask a blessing?"

"Please do." Caitlyn clasped her hands on the napkin in her lap.

Sarah bowed her head. "Father, we ask You to remember Ali today, and all the other children who need Your love. Guide us to help him. Bless this food, and use us to further Your will. Amen."

"Amen," Caitlyn echoed softly, touched.

"Have you heard any more about how Ali is doing?" Sarah asked as she passed salt and pepper.

"We had a report yesterday from Dr. Mike saying he's

stable and gaining strength." She realized Sarah might not know who Dr. Mike was. "That's Major Mike Montgomery, the army doctor who's been looking after him."

Sarah nodded, her expression clouding. "Yes. I know Dr. Mike."

"That's right, I'd forgotten that Steve said he was stationed here at Fort Bonnell before he went overseas. Were you friends then?"

Sarah put down her fork, the food on it untasted. "You could say that. We were engaged."

"Sarah, I'm sorry. I didn't know." She wasn't sure what to say. This was obviously a delicate subject, and she had stumbled onto it, oblivious.

Sarah forced a smile. "It just didn't work out. That happens. It's best just to part as friends and go on with your lives."

"I guess you're right."

But there was something in Sarah's eyes that said she wasn't over Mike as completely as she proclaimed. Maybe that explained why she was still single.

At least Sarah had loved someone, even if it hadn't worked out. She couldn't say the same for herself.

She'd been so busy with her career that she'd never taken the time for a relationship, even one that ended badly. What did that say about her?

"Catch a fish, win a prize!" Steve shouted, working the fishing game designed for the youngest participants in the charity carnival. Naturally, everyone who tried the game won a prize. Thanks to the generosity of local merchants, he had a huge carton filled with small toys to hand out.

He'd been constantly busy since the carnival opened, and the intensity didn't show any signs of lessening. The cement-block walls of the gym were decorated with bright, colorful posters of the work Children of the Day did around the world.

A steady stream of people still came through the gym doors, and the roar of talk and laughter seemed to shake the rafters. Prairie Springs was turning out in force to support its favorite charity.

There were a good number of folks from Fort Bonnell, as well. That turnout pleased him. A bit of friction naturally existed between the small town and the giant army post that dwarfed it, with the usual stress of soldiers getting into trouble when they were off post. Having soldiers support local events brought a positive balance.

"Hey, Chaplain, how are you?"

The man who halted in front of the fishing booth looked like a typical rancher in jeans, western boots and a plaid shirt, but Steve had known Evan Patterson since even before he wore army green.

"Hey, Evan." He grabbed Evan's hand. "This can't be your little Paige! How did she get so big since the last time I saw her?"

The little girl with Evan smiled proudly, clasping both hands on the edge of the fishing trough. "I'm five," she announced proudly. "I'm going to go to kindergarten pretty soon."

"I guess you will, sugar."

The child's smile touched his heart. Big hazel eyes, tousled blondish-brown hair—Paige looked a lot like her daddy, and judging by the way she looked at him, she adored him.

Evan hadn't had an easy time of it since his wife left them, but he sure was doing a good job of loving that little girl.

"Reckon she better have a few tries with that fishing net of yours."

Evan handed over a bill. Steve gave him the net, and Evan put it in his daughter's hands. "Pick out a good one, now, honey."

Paige watched the plastic fish bob past with big eyes. It looked as if she'd be awhile deciding which to catch.

Steve leaned against the counter, glad to catch up with a man who'd stood beside him during some of the roughest days of his life. They ought to get together more often, and he felt a bit guilty about that. Just because Evan lived out of town on his ranch was no reason to fall out of touch.

"How's your sister doing since she was deployed?"

"Whitney sounds fine, but then, she would." Evan's expression said that they both knew what it was like in a war zone. They'd spent a lot of time there together. "I hear she's been getting letters from Betty Villard's granddaughters."

Steve nodded. "They're in Olga's grief program at the church, and I understand she set it up."

"Rough, what happened to those little girls." Evan glanced protectively at his daughter. "I guess it's really the aunt who's doing the writing for them. They must be about my daughter's age, since they're in her Sunday-school class."

Paige looked up from her preoccupation with the fish. "Who, Daddy? Who's in my Sunday-school class?"

"Amanda and Josie," Steve supplied the names. "Do you know them?"

"Sure. They're twins. I wish I had a twin."

That was one thing her doting father couldn't possibly supply. Steve pointed to a pair of yellow fish. "Those two look like twins. Why not see if you can catch both of them."

With a fair amount of splashing, she managed to get both fish into the net. "I did it, Daddy!"

"You sure did, sweetheart."

"That means you get a prize. Two prizes, as a matter of fact." Steve took the dripping fish and reached into his box. "How about a doll and a crown?"

"Wow!" She plopped the plastic tiara on her head and clutched the small plastic doll. "Thank you."

"You're welcome." He looked up, and his heart gave a little lurch. "Hey, Evan, here's Caitlyn Villard and the twins now. You folks ought to meet each other."

He waved. The twins, spotting him, came running.

Evan's eyes widened appreciatively as Caitlyn came up to the booth. Well, no wonder. She looked great in a pair of white slacks and a shirt the color of strawberry ice cream.

The twins were distracted from him by the sight of Evan's daughter and her prizes, giving him a moment to perform introductions.

"Caitlyn, this is Evan Patterson. He owns a ranch just outside of town, and his daughter, Paige, is in the twins' Sunday-school class. His kid sister, Whitney, is one of the soldiers the twins are writing to."

"How nice to meet you. I didn't realize Whitney had family locally." Caitlyn shook hands, looking up at Evan with a warm smile. "Her e-mails to the twins have been so interesting."

Evan propped his hand on the counter and smiled down at her. "You folks are probably hearing from her more often than I am. I haven't had an e-mail in a couple of days. What's she been telling you?"

It wouldn't be fair to say that Evan was putting on the charm. He was just a naturally friendly, laid-back guy—or at least he had been before his wife broke his heart. It was a good sign that he was ready to smile at a pretty girl, wasn't it?

"She writes about camp life, what they have to eat, the children that she sees in the village. Anything she thinks will interest a couple of five-year-olds, I suppose."

Evan looked at the girls, who were chattering away excitedly. "Will you listen to that? How about if we walk these three around together for a bit? You can tell me how you're enjoying Prairie Springs."

Caitlyn shot a look toward Steve, as if wanting his advice.

"Sure, why don't you do that," he said. Well, what else could he say? Evan was a good ole boy, and he sure didn't have any claim on Caitlyn. "Go ahead."

"Fine. Thanks." She smiled at Evan. "We'll see you later, Steve."

"See you," he echoed, and watched the five of them walk off together.

That was good, he told himself. He wasn't emotionally free to love anybody, and Caitlyn deserved a little happiness.

So why did he feel like giving his fish pond a good hearty kick?

The carnival was finally winding down, and as much fun as it had been, Caitlyn was just as glad to see it come to an end. Mama had taken charge of the twins so she could work the cotton-candy stand. After all this excitement, the twins were probably overtired and long past ready to go home.

She was, too. At the moment, all she could think of was that she wanted to stand in a hot shower for about an hour or two. There was cotton candy in her hair, and she'd begun to think she'd never get the smell of sugar out of her system.

All around her, people were closing down their stands. Tired adults lugged even more exhausted children toward the exit, more than a few of the little ones crying out of sheer fatigue and overexcitement. They'd be lucky to get the twins home without a bout of tears.

Still, the children had enjoyed themselves. The twins had spent over an hour with Evan's little girl, making her realize how good it was for them to have someone else to play with besides each other.

It would probably help both of them if she made more of an effort to have that happen. She'd have to check with Mama about the possibility of setting up a play date, maybe with Evan's daughter and a few other children from Sunday school. It could help Josie get out from under Amanda's shadow, and probably other kids wouldn't let Amanda boss them around the way she did her sister.

Evan had certainly been easy to talk to, with none of the undercurrents she felt so strongly when she was with Steve. And he'd been a font of information.

Evan obviously thought highly of Steve. *He was always there, always calm. It seemed like you could just look at him and feel better when everything was going crazy around us.*

She took out her cash box and started to count the money, fairly sure no one would want cotton candy for the trip home.

Steve was a calming influence, all right. But what did he mean by shoving her off on Evan? Was that a not-so-gentle hint that she'd gotten too close to him? The more she thought of it, the more annoyed she became.

And it was Steve's misfortune that he came wandering over to her booth just when she had a good head of steam building.

"Went pretty well, didn't it?" Steve shifted from one foot to the other. "We had even more people than last year. And a news crew interviewed Anna for one of the Austin television stations. That'll be great publicity for COTD."

"Yes, it will." She began shutting down, not looking at him.

"I just wish she could have told those reporters that Ali was on his way." Steve leaned on the counter, apparently not intending to go anywhere very soon.

Still, his comment distracted her from her irritation with him.

"I'm concerned that we're wasting too much time waiting for the general to come to his senses. I'm going to meet with Jake tomorrow to go over alternate plans."

"I guess we have to come up with something." He paused. "You know, Jake's a good ole boy." He wasn't looking at her. "You two should have a lot in common, I'd think, both of you attorneys."

She slammed the door of the cotton-candy machine closed, making him look at her, startled.

"First Evan, now Jake. Will you please stop trying to fix me up with someone?"

"I didn't mean—"

"Oh, yes, you did." She planted her hands on the counter, determined to get this said. "Look, I don't know what's going on with you, but if I want a romance, I'll find my own candidate. Okay?"

He raised his hands in a gesture of surrender. "Sorry. Maybe I was being a tad pushy. Forget it."

"Fine." She snapped the word. She could forget his clumsy matchmaking efforts.

But she couldn't forget that he obviously felt she was leaning on him too much. He was clearly trying to let her know that he was off limits.

Well, fine. He was the one who'd kissed her, after all. But she'd gotten the message now. She wouldn't be weeping on his shoulder again any time soon.

Mama approached through the thinning crowd, pulling two tired girls along by the hand. "I'm going to head for home with these two. Now, don't feel you have to rush home, if you and Steve are talking."

Was her mother attempting a little matchmaking, too? "I'll be home as soon as I can. Believe me, all I want is to take a shower and get to bed."

Amanda tugged on Steve's pant leg. "We're going swimming tomorrow, Chaplain Steve. Why don't you come, too?"

"I'm sure Chaplain Steve has work to do," Caitlyn said quickly. Maybe it was time all of them stopped relying on Steve.

"Tell you what." He squatted down to Amanda's level. "I do have a lot of errands to run tomorrow. But if I can, I'll come by the pool. Okay?"

"Okay." Amanda leaned against her grandmother, obviously too tired even to pester him.

"We're off now." Her mother turned the twins toward the door. "We'll see you later."

"Bye. I'll be home soon." When they were gone, she

turned to Steve. "You don't have to do that. I'm sure you have things to do tomorrow."

"I said I'd try, and I will." He gave her a distant look. "Tomorrow is Carolyn's birthday, isn't it? Did you talk to the girls about that?"

"No. I decided not to bring it up." It was her decision, after all.

"I see."

He sounded annoyed. Well, fine. She was annoyed, too. She'd never felt so out of patience with him before, and right at the moment, she didn't care what he thought of her.

Chapter Twelve

He hadn't been making it up when he'd told the twins that he had a lot of errands to run. Steve trotted across the lawn toward the office wing of Prairie Springs Christian Church, intent on crossing a few more things off his list before the day grew any older.

He and Pastor Frank were cosponsoring a visiting missionary in September, and plans were already well under way. He just needed to check a few details on the arrangements with Frank so that he could send out a letter to the speaker.

As he reached the door, he spotted Olga Terenkov rounding the corner from the rear parking lot. She juggled what seemed to be a hot casserole dish, in addition to the oversize embroidered tote bag she always carried. She looked as if she could use a hand.

He smiled as she drew closer. Olga's denim skirt, cowgirl boots and the Stetson topping her blond hair announced the enormous pride she took in being a Texan. With a Russian accent.

"You've got your hands full." He swung the door open. "Any chance you want me to carry that?"

"I can manage, Steve, but thank you. How nice it is to see you today. I didn't have a chance to talk to you last night because I was so busy in the kitchen."

"And I was so busy with the fish pond, I never had a chance to eat." He followed her into the hallway. "We did pretty well, I hear."

Olga beamed. "The most we've ever made from the carnival. A Texas-size turnout, wasn't it? People are so kind."

"They sure are." He sniffed. "That smells like your special perogies. How about inviting me to share lunch with you?"

Olga's gaze slid away from his. "They are not for my lunch. But I promise, I'll make some for you another day." She paused in front of her office door, fumbling for keys in that oversize bag.

He took the casserole dish so she could find them. "You brought this to take to someone in need?" He did a quick mental inventory of folks on the prayer list he and Frank shared.

"No, not exactly." To his astonishment, Olga's fair skin flushed bright pink. "I brought them as a treat for Franklin."

"Franklin," he repeated. "It's not his birthday, is it?"

"No." The blush deepened. She turned away, hustling into her tiny office.

He followed her, setting the casserole dish on top of the bookcase where she indicated. Olga was a generous soul, always giving to people. What was there about bringing food to Frank to merit that blush? The answer that occurred to him had him staring at her, dumbfounded.

"Olga, is there something I should know about going on between you and Frank?"

"No. Yes." Suddenly Olga looked like the girl she must have been, caught between laughter and tears. "It is so foolish at my age, but I cannot help it. I have feelings for him."

He stared at her in consternation. Feelings for Frank Fields? That was a shocker.

"I know, I know what you are going to say. That I am too old for such things." Olga's Russian accent was becoming more pronounced as she spoke, a sure sign of emotion.

"That's not what I was going to say at all." He spoke slowly, feeling his way, anxious not to hurt her by his reaction. "But Franklin Fields—does he return your feelings?"

She shrugged extravagantly. "Who can tell with him, he hides his feelings so well. We have been friends and colleagues for such a long time. He probably doesn't think of me any other way."

"But you think of him that way." This didn't seem like a situation that would end well.

Olga fidgeted with the set of Russian nesting dolls on the table. "I didn't expect to. After Anna's father died in Afghanistan, I never expected to love anyone again. But sometimes love can surprise you."

The words seemed to resonate inside him, and he tried to shake them off.

"All this time I work with Frank."

Olga's usually firm grasp of English grammar was deserting her in her excitement, and Steve realized he was probably the only person she'd confided this in, which put an even bigger burden on him to handle it delicately.

"I admire and respect him, nothing more. But one day

he turns and looks at me and *poof!* Just like that, I knew I loved him."

He had to speak. He couldn't let Olga walk right into disaster without trying to head her off.

"Olga, you know I love you."

She swung toward him, patting his cheek. "And I you. You are a dear boy."

"I just think—well, I'm afraid that Frank isn't looking for romance."

He shook his head, feeling as if he heard an echo. Wasn't that what Caitlyn had said to him last night?

"Well, of course not." She smiled fondly. "I know he is not looking for a new love. But if only I can break through that reserve of his, I am sure that he will see he cares for me, too."

"Olga, darlin'—" He took her hands in his. He'd have to tell her what he knew to be true. "Listen to me. Franklin doesn't want it generally known, but before he came here to Prairie Springs, he suffered a terrible personal loss. I don't want you to get hurt, but I'm afraid he's just not open to love."

Olga just looked at him for a long moment, her wide blue eyes slowly filling with tears.

"I'm sorry." He felt like a heel for telling her, but what else could he do?

"I am sorry, too." Making an obvious effort to control herself, she patted his hands. "Because I think, you know, that you are not just talking about Frank. You are talking about yourself, too."

Even sitting in the hot sunshine at the pool watching the twins take their swimming lesson, Caitlyn felt as if she were stuck under a dark cloud that pressed down on her, filling her with dread.

She leaned back in the lounge chair and tried to think about something—anything—other than the fact that today was Carolyn's birthday. And Carolyn was gone.

Dead. She used the word deliberately in her mind. No more euphemisms about it. Carolyn was dead, and anything that had been left unsaid between them would go forever unspoken.

She tried to focus on Amanda's efforts to conquer swimming on her back, but her mother's wistful words kept intruding. If only she and Carolyn had had the time to get to know one another as adults. They might have learned to be friends.

But they hadn't, and there was no going back.

There was no going back to the events of the previous night, either. Each time she thought of Steve's attitude toward her at the carnival, she became more upset.

What did he mean by trying to fix her up with someone, as if they were back in high school? She certainly wasn't interested in either Evan or Jake, as nice as they were, because she—

Well, she'd better not go there, either. Admitting that she had feelings, deep feelings, for Steve would only lead to heartbreak.

Maybe she should accept the fact that this was going to be a difficult day on all fronts, and let it go at that.

Mama would no doubt spend the afternoon crying. When they got home, she'd pretend nothing was wrong, but they'd all know there was. She'd try to ignore Mama's red eyes and keep the girls from making some comment.

Her throat tightened at the thought. Would it have been better to discuss Carolyn's birthday out in the open? She just didn't know.

Amanda, giving up on the backstroke, had decided to splash a little boy who was doing better at it than she had. Caitlyn started to get up, but the swim teacher had already intervened.

That was a relief. Amanda had to be corrected, obviously, but she didn't want to have to punish her today, of all days. She leaned back just as a tall shadow loomed across the hot white concrete.

She knew without turning to see who it was. She must be pretty far gone, if she recognized him without even looking.

Steve paused for a moment, not speaking, the shadow perfectly still. Then he dragged a chair over next to her, the metal base shrieking on the concrete, and sat down.

She turned to study his face, grateful that she could hide behind the cover of her dark sunglasses.

Today he looked distracted. Sober, with the usual easy smile gone from his eyes.

"I'm sorry," he said abruptly. "I owe you an apology for last night. I was out of line."

She waited for more, but apparently that was all he had to say on the subject.

"It's all right," she said, when the silence had stretched on too long. "Don't worry about it."

But it wasn't all right, not really. Steve had had some reason for his sudden attempt to interest her in other men. Either he didn't know himself what that was, or he wasn't willing to say it to her. He couldn't be honest with her about his feelings. There was nothing she could do about that.

He leaned his elbows on his knees, hands linked loosely. Instead of swim trunks he wore his usual uniform, so he evidently didn't intend to stay. The afternoon sunlight brought out golden highlights in his hair.

She wanted to brush that hair back away from his eyes, soothe away the worry lines that crinkled his forehead. But she couldn't.

Maybe a change of subject would restore a measure of peace between them. Steve obviously only wanted to be friends with her, so she'd talk to him casually, as a friend.

"Did you get all your errands accomplished?"

"What?" For a moment he didn't seem to know what she was talking about. "Oh, that. Yes, I did."

But the mention seemed to make him more distracted instead of less.

She sighed, turning her attention to the twins. The lesson was over, so the children were enjoying some free play in the pool. At least, she supposed enjoy was the right word. There was a lot of shouting and splashing going on, their high voices echoing shrilly as the kids played. Some of the waiting mothers were already pulling out beach bags and gathering scattered belongings, getting ready to leave.

Amanda pulled herself out of the pool and stood on the edge for a moment. "Look at me, look at me, everybody!" She jumped in, splashing everyone within reach.

Caitlyn bit her lip. Should she go and correct her now, or hope that was a onetime outburst that could be ignored?

Amanda jumped up and down in waist-deep water, splashing Josie unmercifully. Josie backed away, holding out her hands in a futile effort to stem the tide.

"Scaredy-cat, scaredy-cat. You're too scared to jump in the water."

Josie began to cry. Caitlyn swung her legs off the lounge chair and reached the edge of the pool a step ahead of Steve.

"Amanda Susan Mayhew. You come out of the pool this instant."

Amanda looked so startled at Caitlyn's tone that she froze for a moment. Then, pouting, she trudged through the water to the steps. She climbed out, her lower lip jutting.

She stopped a few feet in front of Caitlyn, planting her hands on her hips. "I didn't do anything."

"You teased your sister." She tried to keep her voice calm and matter-of-fact. "You jumped off the edge of the pool, which you know isn't allowed. Now sit down on that chair until I tell you to get up."

"I don't want a time-out!" Amanda stamped a bare, wet foot on the concrete. "I don't."

"Too bad. You earned it. Now sit."

Amanda blinked. Then, lower lip protruding, she stamped across to the chair and sat, folding her arms in mute protest.

The overacting was so blatant that Caitlyn had to fight to suppress a grin. She caught Steve's gaze and saw that he had the same reaction. She bit her lip, averting her face so that Amanda wouldn't see her.

But Amanda was staring at something in the distance, her mouth open.

"Auntie Caitlyn, look! Josie!"

She turned in the direction Amanda pointed. Her heart stopped as a wave of sheer terror washed over her.

Josie was three-quarters of the way up the ladder that led to the high dive, climbing steadily.

Caitlyn wasn't sure how she got to the base of the high dive. She just knew she was there, gripping the ladder, with Steve right beside her.

"Josie," she called the name, trying to keep panic out of her voice.

Josie turned just enough to look at her, clinging to the railings. Her small face was set.

"Please, sweetheart, come down."

Josie shook her head.

"Josie, come down now."

But Josie reached upward. Her hand missed the railing. Her little body wobbled, swinging out from the stairs.

Someone gasped. Caitlyn kept her eyes on Josie, as if she could pin the child to the ladder by the force of her gaze.

After a seemingly endless moment Josie grasped the railing.

She could breathe again. Somehow, she had to stay calm. Upsetting Josie would only make matters worse.

"Josie, that's enough. You almost fell. Come back down here."

Josie climbed up another step. Then she paused and looked down again. "I can't. I'm going to jump off the high dive like Mommy did."

"No, Josie. No."

No answer. In that moment, as she listened for a response, she realized that the whole area had gone perfectly silent. The lifeguards had cleared the pool already. Even now they moved into place around the edge of the deep end, ready to dive into the pool the instant Josie hit the water.

Terror gripped her like a physical thing, a vise tightening on the back of her neck. Hitting the water from that height would be bad enough. What if Josie lost her grip before she reached the platform? For an instant she seemed to see her falling, falling…

"I have to go up after her."

Steve caught her hand, trying to pull it off the railing. "No, Caitlyn. Let me. I know you hate heights. Let me do it."

She stared at him. Steve meant well, but he didn't understand.

"I have to. The twins are my responsibility. I have to go."

She turned back to the ladder, grabbed the railing and started climbing.

The metal railings scorched her hands, but she held on tight. *Don't look up, don't look down, just keep going.* If she let herself think, she might panic.

Please, Lord, please, Lord. Let me be in time. Let me say the right thing.

Other people were praying, too. She could almost feel their prayers, helping to lift her up the ladder.

Steve, too. He would be praying.

Hear us, Father. Protect Your child.

Her sandal caught, and her foot nearly slid out of it. She stumbled, caught herself, her heart pounding erratically. She stood still for a moment.

Breathe. Don't look down. Breathe.

She had to get rid of the sandals before they tripped her up entirely. Holding onto the railing, she shook off the right one. Down, down…she finally heard it hit. She wouldn't think about how far it was. Then the left one.

Her toes clung to the rubber matting on the steps. That was better. She could move faster.

Climb, don't look down. What was the song she and Carolyn had sung at church camp so many times?

We are climbing Jacob's ladder…

Please, Father…

And she was at the top. Her breath caught. Josie stood at the edge of the platform, looking down at the water far below. Air, nothing but thin air surrounded her little body, and the slightest waver could send her over.

Carefully. Don't scare her.

Caitlyn sat down on the platform, swinging her legs around until she had the railing's post at her back. It gave her the faint illusion of stability.

"Josie," she said softly. "Come here, sweetie."

Nothing. Not even a shake of the head.

Keep your voice calm and conversational. Don't give way to the panic, or she might panic, too.

"It makes me dizzy to watch you standing there. Take a step back toward me, okay?"

A moment passed, then another.

Finally Josie took a cautious step backward. Her small figure in her pink-and-white polka-dot swimsuit was very straight.

I want you in my arms, baby. Don't you understand that?

"What are you doing up here?" She forced herself to sound relaxed.

"It's Mommy's birthday today." Josie's voice was matter-of-fact. "I'm going to jump off the high dive like she did."

Her throat clutched, and she had to clear it before she could speak. "You know, I remember the first time your mommy went off the high dive," she said. "I was here that day, watching her. She was eleven. That's six whole years older than you are."

Josie's head turned slightly, as if to say she was listening.

"You know, I don't think Mommy would want you to jump off when you're five. I think she'd want you to wait until you're older, like she did."

No response, and her mind raced, trying to find another argument that the child would heed.

"Mommy was a soldier, and she always followed the rules, remember?"

A nod this time.

"Well, the rules are that no one's allowed to climb the high dive without the lifeguard's permission. And you don't have that, do you?"

Josie shook her head. Slowly, slowly she turned around. Her face was white, her eyes huge and dark. "Manda said I was a scaredy-cat."

Her heart twisted. "Manda didn't mean it, sugar. Sometimes sisters tease each other or say things that hurt each other's feelings, but they don't really mean it. Your mommy and I did that when we were little, you know. Just like you and Amanda."

Josie took a step toward her, her face lightening a bit. "You did?"

"Yes, we did." She could almost breathe, now that Josie had moved toward her. "You and Amanda are a lot like your mommy and I were when we were little."

"I didn't know that."

Her heart hurt. Josie didn't know that because she never talked about Carolyn with her.

"I'm sorry, Josie. I think you wanted to talk about

Mommy's birthday, and I didn't let you because it made me sad. And Amanda's being mean because she's sad. And you climbed up here because you're sad."

She took a breath, sent up another silent, fervent prayer.

"Wouldn't it be better if we could just be sad together, instead? I really need you to give me a hug right now."

She held out her arms. With a choked sob, Josie ran into them.

Caitlyn held her close, her tears spilling over. *Thank You, Father. Thank You.*

Chapter Thirteen

Steve couldn't help himself. He had to run over to Caitlyn's that evening, just to be sure everything was all right with her and the children.

Every time he thought about how dangerous Josie's adventure had been, chills gripped his spine, and he sensed again the helplessness he'd felt as he'd watched Caitlyn climb that ladder after her.

Thank You, Father. You surely were with us in our trial today.

He'd been murmuring that prayer for hours, but it still seemed he hadn't said it enough.

Us. He couldn't help putting himself with Caitlyn and the children, either. Somehow, that fact made it seem that a relationship between him and Caitlyn wasn't so impossible after all. Maybe he was finally going to put the past behind him.

If he could.

He'd insisted on driving Caitlyn and the twins home after the incident, while the shaken swim teacher followed in his car. Caitlyn had seemed…

He paused, thinking about her reactions.

Okay, he supposed, all things considered. She'd climbed back down the ladder with Josie as if she'd never even thought of being afraid of the height. Her attention and concern was all for the children, without a thought left for him.

Well, that was what he'd wanted, wasn't it? He'd asked God to use him to bring her and the twins together. He hadn't expected it to happen quite so dramatically, but it seemed to him she was on her way now.

If that was all that came out of his relationship with her, if there wasn't going to be anything else, then he had to be content with that.

He parked at the curb and crossed to the wide front porch of Betty's house. He'd never felt quite so indecisive in his life, and he didn't like it.

He knocked on the door, glancing at his watch. It was later than he'd thought. The twins were probably already in bed.

Caitlyn opened the door. Her face was drawn with exhaustion. Maybe he should have just called.

"I probably shouldn't have come. I wanted to be sure y'all are okay."

Caitlyn glanced behind her. "I just got the girls settled. If they hear your voice, they'll be up again. Do you mind if we sit out here?"

"Not at all, but you don't have to take the time for me if you'd rather just relax."

She shook her head. "It's okay."

He held the screen door as she came out and followed her to the porch swing. This time he sat down next to her instead of shying away, as he had the last time they'd sat out here.

"They're okay," she said, her breath coming out in a sigh. She collapsed back against the cushions, as if the effort to stay upright was just too much.

"Difficult time?"

She managed a faint smile. "You know, I honestly think Amanda was more upset about what happened than Josie was. Mama and I took turns reassuring first one, then the other. Then just when we thought we'd gotten them both calmed down, someone would start to cry, and we'd have to do it all over again."

"I hope your mother wasn't too upset." Betty had been through too much in recent months to have to deal with more anxiety.

"Less so than I'd have thought. She says that after raising the two of us, she's used to kids trying to damage themselves." A shiver went through her. "I'm just glad she wasn't there to see it. That would have been far worse."

He touched her hand lightly. "What about you? How are you?"

Her forehead wrinkled. "How am I? I feel as if God picked me up, turned me around and put me back down again."

He hesitated, wondering how much to say. "Seems to me after an experience like that, a person might see things a bit different."

"Yes." For a moment he thought she wouldn't go on, but then her eyes met his candidly. "I get it now. What you were trying to help me understand. I love them. They're my responsibility for life."

Something that had been taut inside him seemed to ease. "Congratulations. You're a parent."

"Not a very good one."

"Don't say that. It's natural to worry about it, but you shouldn't. You'll do fine."

"I didn't do so fine dealing with Carolyn's birthday, did I?" She pressed her hand against the base of her neck, as if tension had tightened the muscles.

"You handled it the way you thought was best for the girls."

Maybe, if she'd taken his advice, Josie wouldn't have been up on that high dive today. But if so, maybe Caitlyn wouldn't have come to this realization about the children. God had a plan that he wasn't privy to, obviously, and sometimes the things that looked the worst turned out to be for the best.

"But I was wrong." The words seemed to burst out of her. "I was wrong. I should have talked to them about Carolyn's birthday, and I took the coward's way out. Is it always going to be this hard?"

He could hear the pain that lay beneath the words, and he wanted to do something to ease the hurt, but he knew he couldn't, not really. "You're still learning, so give yourself a pass on a few mistakes. Anyway, I guess kids can always come up with new ways to try their parents, even very experienced ones."

"With me the twins get inexperience." She managed a smile. "But I guess we can learn together."

He hesitated. He didn't want to bring up something else painful, but if not now, when would he ever do it? "I've been thinking that it might help your relationship with the girls if you dealt with your own unresolved feelings about your sister."

Her face tightened. "There's nothing to resolve. Carolyn's gone."

"Carolyn's gone, and you're angry with her for dying."

She shook her head. "You may be right, but I'm just too tired to analyze my own grief right now."

He couldn't seem to leave it alone. "If you could just deal with your own grief—"

She shot off the swing so abruptly that it shook. "Don't, Steve."

He stood, too, his heart wrenching with pity for her. "I'm sorry. I'm just trying to help."

"Help?" She echoed the word. "How can you help me deal with my grief? You know, I had it right the first time when I said you didn't understand. You try to help everyone else, when the truth is that you haven't even dealt with your own grief yet."

He stood there for a moment, feeling as if she'd slapped him. Then he turned and walked away, leaving her all alone.

Caitlyn hung up the phone in her office and pushed back from her desk, feeling as if she'd been hit with a sledgehammer. This Monday had been difficult enough without a pressure-filled call from her boss back in New York about her continued absence.

She ran her fingers through her hair. Coffee, she needed coffee. It would clear her mind. Too bad it wouldn't work that well on her heart.

She'd been busy kicking herself since snapping at Steve. She'd spoken out of her own hurt and exhaustion, but that didn't excuse it.

She'd started to call him a dozen times on Sunday, but each time she'd backed away. Maybe she shouldn't have said the words, but she knew in her heart they were true.

Steve was counseling other people with their grief, but he had yet to deal with his own. The proof of that was in the way he'd walked away without a word.

She crossed the office and headed down the hall toward the kitchen, where surely there would be some coffee brewing. Maybe she ought to concentrate on her job problems, although they seemed almost as intractable as Steve.

Olga was already standing at the coffeemaker, pouring a mug. After one look at Caitlyn's face, she handed it to her.

"You are in need of this much more than I am," she said.

"Thanks." She put a spoonful of sugar into the mug while Olga fixed another for herself. "I guess I need something to wake me up this morning."

Olga took her arm and led her to a seat at the table, sitting down next to her. "It is more than waking up that's the problem, I think."

She stared down at her coffee, unwilling to open her mouth about any of her problems for fear too much would come spilling out.

Olga patted her hand. "I won't say anything to anyone. That's part of being a counselor, whether we're in my office or at the kitchen table."

She thought of Steve, unable to tell her about General Willis no matter how much he'd wanted to. Olga, too, had her code.

"Life just seems so difficult right now." The temptation to pour it out to a sympathetic ear was too strong. "My firm back in New York is putting pressure on me to go back."

"That bothers you." Olga's voice was warm and caring.

"I thought I'd have more time. The twins—there's so

much still to be done here. And besides, there's Ali. I have a responsibility to him, too."

"Responsibilities in many directions, it seems. That makes it hard to decide which is most important."

Something in her bristled at that. Would she really say that her career was more important than the twins? Of course she wouldn't.

"The girls come first. They have to."

Olga nodded. "It makes decisions easier when you know what comes first."

"It's not as simple as that." If it were, she wouldn't be struggling. "Frankly, I can make a lot more money back in New York."

"And the twins need money."

"Well, no, but—" She shook her head. "All right, I get it. When I talk about going back, it's for my sake, not theirs."

Olga smiled. "I wouldn't put it so harshly, but yes, I think that's so."

"Fair enough, but I can't spend the rest of my life in Prairie Springs."

Olga's eyebrows shot up. "What is wrong with Prairie Springs?"

Caitlyn couldn't help but smile at the expression on her face. "Nothing. Everything. I spent eighteen years of my life preparing to leave this place."

"And I spent many more years of my life preparing to be here!" Olga threw up her hands in an extravagant gesture.

"You're an adopted Texan," she said. "You chose this life."

"Of course! I love it here. I love all things Texas—the size, the people, the friendliness that just wraps around you." She smiled slyly. "And the wonderful men. Like Steve."

The name pricked her heart. "Now, Olga, don't tell me you have a crush on him."

"He is a sweet boy, but no, I do not. I think perhaps he is interested in you."

Not anymore. She shook her head. "Don't try to matchmake for me. I'm not in the market."

"Why not? He would be a wonderful father for the twins, besides being perfect for you."

"I'm not interested." Did Olga know what a fib that was? She sought for a way to divert Olga's attention from her love life. "Anyway, you should be looking for a romance of your own. You're still youthful, beautiful and so full of life. Isn't there some cowboy we can lasso for you?"

To her surprise, Olga's blue eye grew serious at the question. "I am, as the saying goes, into someone who's just not into me."

"Olga, I'm sorry." She clasped Olga's hand, wondering who on earth her mystery man could be. "I shouldn't have said anything."

"It's all right." She seemed to look off into space for a moment, perhaps envisioning the man of her dreams. Then she shook her head. "It is probably for the best. Anna wouldn't like me to date, anyway."

"I'm sure—" she began, and then censored herself. How did she know how Anna would react at the thought of her mother dating?

"Yes, it is best." But the sorrow in Olga's voice made Caitlyn long to do something to make the situation better for her.

"You know, mothers and daughters, no matter how much they love each other, can struggle sometimes." Her own relationship with her mother had certainly changed and deepened since she'd come home. "Anna might be bothered at first, but maybe she just needs help seeing you in a new light."

"Maybe," Olga said, her tone doubtful. She patted Caitlyn's hand. "I'll tell you what, little Caitlyn. I will pray for you, and you will pray for me. And maybe our Father will show us the answers for both of us."

"I hope so." She really did, although she suspected that her faith wasn't nearly as strong as Olga's.

"Caitlyn, come in," Anna's voice called as Caitlyn tapped at the French door in response to a message that Anna wanted to see her.

She pushed open the door and came face-to-face with Steve. For a moment she couldn't speak—couldn't even breathe.

Finally she managed a nod. "Hi, Steve." Her voice sounded strained, even to her.

Steve's smile was more of a grimace. Well, what could she expect? She responded to his concern for her family by slapping him in the face with his own grief.

"Come over here, you two." Anna didn't seem to notice anything wrong. "Dr. Mike is calling any minute now, and he wants to talk to all of us."

"Is something wrong?" She turned toward the desk, glad to have something to distract her from Steve's presence. He took a step back, gesturing for her to go first.

Anna shrugged, spreading her hands in a movement that reminded Caitlyn of Olga. "I guess we'll find out as soon as his call comes through."

Steve followed her to the desk. "I wish we had more progress to report on Ali's situation."

He sounded more natural now, and Caitlyn felt as if she could breathe again.

"Here he comes." Anna came to attention behind her computer, and they hurried around the desk.

Steve pulled a chair over for her and then stood behind it. She was very aware of his hands braced on its back, inches from her shoulders.

Dr. Mike's face came into focus on the screen against a background of what looked like a mud wall.

Anna adjusted the microphone. "It's good to see you, Mike. How are things there?"

There was a pause before his voice came through. "A little quieter, thank the good Lord for that. What's going on with you folks? You make any progress with General Willis yet?"

"I wish we had." Steve leaned forward between the chairs, speaking quickly as if to take the brunt of their failure upon himself. "We've tried everything we can think of, but he's refusing even to see us."

Dr. Mike shook his head, and Caitlyn's heart sank at the seriousness of his expression. They were going to hear something bad—she knew it.

"How is Ali?" Anna said urgently, as if she'd gotten the same message. "Is something wrong?"

"The situation isn't critical," he said. "Yet. But Ali is not improving the way we'd hoped he would. It's beginning to look as if his condition isn't going to resolve itself."

"You're saying he doesn't have much time left." Anna's tone was clear.

"I wouldn't put it quite that bluntly." Mike gave them a tired smile. "But the sooner we get him someplace that's prepared to do pediatric cardiac surgery, the better off he's going to be. If he should have a crisis here, we're just not equipped to handle it."

"It's so frustrating." Caitlyn's hands clenched. "The child is an American citizen. There has to be a way we can get him here."

"Has Jake Hopkins been able to come up with anything?" Steve put the question so cautiously that she knew he was remembering her anger at his attempt to push her toward the attorney.

"He's not very hopeful," she admitted. "If we can't get the cooperation of a relative, and that means the general, our next best bet is a diplomatic intervention. He spoke to you about it, didn't he, Anna?"

She nodded. "I've been contacting everyone I can think of. We've had some encouragement, but nothing solid yet."

Mike frowned. "There's no way to have the foundation take responsibility for Ali?"

"Jake says not." Caitlyn hated admitting that, and she could feel Anna's frustration in the way her hands gripped the edge of the desk. "Children of the Day simply doesn't have any standing in the case, not legally, anyway. State law says we need a relative."

She glanced at Steve. He'd fallen silent just when she'd expected his comments. He seemed to be staring at the computer screen without seeing it, as three vertical lines appeared between his brows.

She nudged him. "Any suggestions?"

He looked at her as if she were a stranger, and blinked,

turning back to the screen. "Mike, do you think you can get us some video clips of Ali?"

Mike's eyebrows lifted in surprise. "Yes, I guess so. One of the nurses who is stationed here has been showing off a new camera. In fact, she might have already taken some footage of Ali."

"Can you get it to us as soon as possible? It doesn't have to be anything lengthy or elaborate. Just something that shows what he looks like—maybe have him say a few words in English if possible."

"You're thinking about what Miss Willis said," Caitlyn observed. She glanced from Anna to Mike's image. "She talked to us about how proud the general was of Greg, and she said that the general was always showing her pictures and movies of him." She felt a tentative excitement beginning to build.

Steve nodded, a smile touching his face, and she realized they were looking at each other as friends again. "He doesn't want to see us. I wonder how he'd react to seeing his grandson?"

"I hate to put a damper on the idea, but how are we going to get him to watch it?"

He gave her that easy, lopsided grin that never failed to touch her heart. "That part is still to be worked out," he admitted. "But I think we might be able to get some help from Miss Willis."

"I know she'd do anything she could." Her excitement rose to match his. For a moment, as their eyes met, it was as if they were the only ones there.

Her breath caught as her heart seemed to go into a spasm. How long was this going to hurt so much?

Chapter Fourteen

"He's coming. I can see his car pulling into the driveway. Are you ready?" Miss Willis, her wheelchair pulled up to the side window of her brother's study, swung around toward them, her face bright with anticipation.

Steve nodded, though what he was feeling was closer to dread. They were about to confront the general for what would undoubtedly be their last chance.

He glanced at Caitlyn, who stood next to the table on which they'd placed the laptop computer he'd brought. Her hands twisted together.

"We're as ready as we'll ever be, I guess," he said, trying to smile.

Miss Willis gave a nod and wheeled herself out into the middle of the room. She obviously intended that she be the first person General Willis saw when he entered the room.

That was for the best, although they hadn't really considered that when they made their plans. At least that would buy them a couple of brief moments while the general reacted to his sister's presence. When he saw them, the fireworks were bound to start.

He could only hope and pray that he wasn't creating an irreparable breach between Miss Willis and her brother by accepting her help in this.

Still, Lydia Willis was as determined, in her own way, as her brother was in his. If anything, that should play to their advantage. They wouldn't even have gotten into the house without her.

Miss Willis had planned their attack, as organized as a general herself. They would arrive at a time when she knew her brother was out on his usual round of activities. He was as regular about his routine as if he were still in the army, she'd declared.

She would tell the housekeeper she'd wait in the study for him. They'd be all ready when he entered the room.

An ambush, Miss Willis had insisted, her eyes sparkling.

He could hear the sound of the front door closing. Then came the faint murmur of voices—obviously the general and his housekeeper. She'd be telling him about his unexpected guests.

Next came footsteps approaching the room, sounding on the tile floor of the hallway in a crisp, military fashion.

There was barely time for one last prayer.

Our Father, we pray for Your guidance now. Open Marlon Willis's heart to hear our words. Open it to love You and to love this child of Yours who needs so much. Amen.

The door opened.

Marlon Willis strode into the room, erect and military. He saw his sister first, and his expression softened in pleasure.

"Lyddie, I didn't expect—" His words cut off abruptly

when he saw who else had invaded his study. "What are you doing here?" he barked.

Before Steve could respond, Miss Willis spoke.

"I invited them, Marlon."

Color mounted in his face. "Well, you can uninvite them. I don't want the two of them in my house."

"You have to listen to them." Miss Willis sounded perfectly calm and composed. "They have something to say to you."

"I already know what they have to say, and I don't want to hear it again. I thought I'd already made that perfectly clear." He divided a glare between Caitlyn and Steve.

It was a look that had probably made many a young lieutenant quake in his boots, but Steve didn't feel even a tremor. He answered to a higher authority than a three-star general.

He should draw the general's fire from his sister. "We have some important information for you, sir."

General Willis's face darkened. "I told you I don't want to hear it. Now get out of my house, both of you, before I call the police."

"I'm sorry, sir, but we can't do that. Not until you've heard what we have to say."

General Willis stared at him for another second. Then he wheeled around. "Then I'll leave. You can find your own way out of my house."

Steve exchanged a startled glance with Caitlyn. That was the one thing they hadn't counted on—that General Willis would walk out on them before they could say anything.

Willis headed for the door, but before he could reach it, his sister wheeled her chair in front of it. Her cheeks bore a pink flush, and her face was set.

"Marlon Willis, I've heard enough of this foolishness.

You will listen to what these young people have to say, and you will behave like the gentleman you were raised to be. I declare, Mama would spin in her grave if she could hear you today."

It was classic big sister scolding little brother, and the fact that they were both white-haired didn't alter the character of the exchange one bit.

"I'm sorry you had to hear this, Lyddie." The general had the grace to look abashed at his sister's lecture, but his face was still scarlet and his breath came in short, explosive gasps. "I don't know what story these two spun to involve you in their shenanigans, but—"

"They told me about Gregory's son."

Silence for a moment. Then he shook his head, for all the world like a bull shaking off flies that were tormenting him. "I don't want to talk about it."

"That doesn't change the truth," Miss Willis declared crisply. "Gregory had a child. That boy is now alone and helpless. You must love him for the sake of Gregory, if not for his own."

He flared up at that. "Gregory made his choice against my wishes. I told him I wouldn't be responsible for the consequences if he didn't listen to me."

"Gregory is dead." She paled a little on the word, but her gaze held his steadily. "This boy is all that is left of him. How can you turn your back on his only child?"

He was still shaking his head, but not with the decision he'd shown before. Steve's fists clenched.

Let it be Your voice he hears, Lord. Help him to listen to You.

"He threw it all away." When he spoke, the general's

words were almost a lament. "All of the plans we made, all of his accomplishments."

"He was a fine boy," Miss Willis said gently. "One of the best."

"I told him a hasty marriage was a mistake. He always listened to me before." His gaze was tormented. "Why wouldn't he listen to me then?"

"Marlon, dear." Her voice was very gentle. "He was a man in love."

"I just wanted him to wait for a few more months. Until his tour was up. To make sure the relationship was genuine. Why couldn't he wait?"

"I know how he felt." Steve was astonished at the sound of his own voice. "Don't you remember what it was like?"

Please, Father, let this be the right thing to say.

The general turned slowly to focus on him. "What do you mean?"

"The first time you're deployed in a battle zone. Don't you remember what that was like?"

"It was a long time ago."

"You don't forget. I was there in the first wave into Iraq. I'll never forget."

The general nodded. "I suppose you're right. You never do forget that."

"It's as clear to me as if it happened yesterday." His throat tightened, and he had to force himself to go on. "The pressure, the uncertainty. The tension of all the soldiers around you. The sense that your life could end at any minute when you see your friends die."

A spasm of some emotion crossed General Willis's face. "That's what it is to be a soldier. Gregory chose that life."

"He followed his father's example," Steve said, "just as I did mine when I became a chaplain. And I know that if you have a chance at happiness when you're in a situation like that, you can't turn away."

He was betraying too much of himself, and Caitlyn was there, listening. But he had no choice. Ali's life depended on what was said in this room today.

The general's face was rigid. Were they getting through to him at all? Only the faintest hum from the computer broke the silence.

"I think I know what Gregory was feeling," Steve said quietly. "I've felt the same thing, too. When you find love in the middle of destruction, it's so rare and beautiful that you can't ignore it."

"You can wait." His voice was harsh.

"No. You can't wait, either, because if you wait, you might lose it." He thought of Elaine and felt as if his heart would break all over again. "Please—" his voice choked, "don't turn your back on your son."

"It's too late." Willis shook his head, and Steve thought there were tears in his eyes. "It's too late. If Gregory had lived—but now it's too late."

"It's not too late."

Steve blinked. He turned to stare at Caitlyn. She was looking at General Willis, not at him.

"It's never too late," she said. "It's never too late to make peace with those we love."

Caitlyn stiffened to bear the weight of the general's stare as he turned toward her. Was she doing the right thing by intervening now? She wasn't sure, but somehow she felt compelled to speak.

"What do you know about it?" His voice was gruff, his gaze frosty.

She swallowed the lump in her throat. "My sister and I weren't as close as sisters should be. I never had the chance to make peace with her."

"It's not the same," he began.

"My sister was a soldier." Caitlyn realized that for the first time, she was saying the words proudly. "Don't you tell me it's not the same. She died in action, along with her husband."

She stared at the general, daring him to make light of her loss in comparison with his.

He didn't move, but it almost seemed that he winced in pain. "I'm sorry for your sacrifice," he said finally.

"I think it's earned me the right to be heard." She held herself upright, her hand pressing against the table.

He jerked a nod of acceptance.

"My sister left five-year-old twin girls," she said. "They're the same age as Ali. I'm responsible for them now."

She thought he was about to speak, so she swept on. She had to get this said while she could, because it had been burning in her the whole time she'd been standing in the general's study, listening to his grief.

"I thought I could ignore my feelings and just go on. But I can't." Her voice shook. "I'm angry with Carolyn, you know that? I'm angry with her for dying and for leaving her children. I'm angry that we never got the chance to be friends as adults. Angry that Carolyn left me to be a parent to those girls when I don't know how."

She took a breath, realizing she felt freer for having said it.

"I don't have the answers yet, but I know now I have to deal with my anger and grief so I can love those children." She took a step toward him, holding out her hand. "Please. Don't let your anger and disappointment get in the way of loving that child."

He didn't respond.

She sagged, reaching behind her to grasp the table. She'd failed, and she didn't have anything left.

"Listen to them," Miss Willis said softly. "This little boy is all that we have left of Gregory."

Still he didn't react. And then Caitlyn realized that there were tears in his eyes. His lips were pressed so tightly together because he had to keep them from trembling.

Now was the time. She glanced at Steve, and he nodded. She switched on the video clip they had set up on the computer.

For a second nothing happened, and she had a moment's fear that she'd messed it up. Then the flap of an army tent appeared on the computer screen.

A hand pushed the tent flap away, and the camera moved inside, to focus on a small figure sitting cross-legged on a cot. The camera zoomed in.

The boy was playing with a toy soldier—one of those little action figures so beloved by little boys. He looked up suddenly, smiling at the camera, and she heard General Willis gasp.

"Hi, Dr. Mike." Ali gave an engaging smile. "See my soldier?"

"That's pretty cool." The voice of the cameraman was Dr. Mike's. "Where did you get him, Ali?"

"One of the nurses, she gave it to me. She say he is like my father."

"He sure is. That was a nice present. Do you remember your daddy?"

Ali's eyes were huge in his thin face. "I remember. He used to sing to me—a funny song about having Texas in his heart."

"I know that one." Mike sounded as if he was having trouble controlling his voice. "Listen, how about saying hello to our friends in Texas? Remember how we practiced it?"

Ali sat up very straight. "I remember." He grinned at the camera. "Howdy, y'all."

The screen went blank.

Caitlyn held her breath. That was it. They'd given everything they had. Would it be enough?

Please, Lord. Please, Lord.

She turned slowly to look at the general.

Tears streamed down his face. "Gregory," he murmured. "He's just like my Gregory."

Steve watched the general. The man had been staring out the window for the past five minutes, struggling to regain his control. He might never forgive them for having seen him weep. Steve could only pray that wouldn't make a difference to his decision.

Miss Willis had pulled her wheelchair up to the coffee table. She placidly drank a glass of sweet tea that she'd told the housekeeper to bring for them, taking control as if this afternoon visit were the most common thing in the world.

Caitlyn had a glass of tea in front of her, too. She'd taken a long drink of it when it was first handed to her. Since then she'd sat in the corner of the leather sofa, looking about as dazed as he felt.

They'd both said things in the past hour that they'd never intended to say. He'd given away too much about his feelings for Elaine—things he wasn't sure he understood himself yet.

The truth was that each time he'd taken a step toward Caitlyn, his memories of Elaine had stopped him. Unless and until he could come to her with a whole heart, he had to stay away.

As for what Caitlyn had said—well, that was what he'd been praying for. If Caitlyn was finally coming to terms with her feelings about her sister, maybe it had all been worth it, whatever the outcome.

Had they succeeded? Surely General Willis would cooperate after his emotional response to the sight of Ali, but still…

Please, Father. I know You've been with us today. Marlon Willis is so close. Please bring him the rest of the way he has to come.

Willis turned from the window, clearing his throat as he stared at them. "Well, why are you all sitting around drinking sweet tea?" he said abruptly. "We should be making plans."

"We're waiting for you, Marlon," Miss Willis said serenely.

"Let's talk strategy." He came toward them, rubbing his hands together, very much the general in control again. "What's our first step to getting my grandson here where he belongs?"

Thank You, Lord. Praise You for this answer to our prayers.

Steve nodded to Caitlyn, trying to emulate the general in controlling his emotion, although he felt like shouting with thanksgiving.

"Caitlyn is the one who has been working with the attorney on the legalities of the situation. She can fill you in."

Caitlyn straightened. "I'm an attorney myself, but since I'm not licensed in Texas, I've been consulting with Jake Hopkins, a local attorney."

That was a wise move, establishing her bona fides. Willis was someone who would respond to that.

"Hopkins is a good man," Willis said. "I've heard him mentioned favorably." He sat down in a leather armchair across from her, apparently ready to listen.

"The process shouldn't be difficult at all," she said, seeming to gain confidence as she went. "Jake will be happy to talk with you about it, but basically, you apply to the court to be Ali's conservator. In that role, you have the right to make decisions about his future. Including, obviously, where he lives and his medical care."

"I'm the boy's grandfather. I should be his guardian, not a conservator, whatever that means."

Obviously now that the general was in, he was in completely.

"You will be, in every way. It's just that applying for conservatorship is the simplest and fastest method of getting Ali to the States, in case he has to have surgery." Caitlyn was quick and incisive now that she was on familiar turf. "Jake will get an emergency hearing with a judge, and under the circumstances, it will be approved very quickly, possibly in a matter of hours. Then you'll have the authority to bring Ali here for good."

He nodded. "Sounds straightforward enough. What about Children of the Day? How do they fit in?"

"We'll be glad to arrange for transport and do anything we can to make things smooth and easy for you and Ali. We already have a pediatric cardiologist on standby in Austin, but if you prefer to make your own arrangements, of course you're free to do that."

"No, no." He waved that suggestion away. "This is your area of expertise."

"Very well." Caitlyn hesitated, and Steve wondered if she was about to express her relief. But she didn't. Maybe she guessed, as he did, that the general would prefer to keep things businesslike. "Jake will get in touch with you sometime today, Chaplain Steve will organize the transportation and I'll alert the medical team."

She rose, and he stood with her.

"Good," the general said gruffly. He hesitated, and then stuck out his hand. "Thank you. All three of you."

Steve didn't know about Caitlyn, but he was about ready to burst with pleasure. He shook hands with the general. Then he bent over Miss Willis, kissing her soft, wrinkled cheek.

"Thank you," he whispered. "We couldn't have done it without you."

She patted his cheek, her eyes sparkling. "We've done a good thing today, all of us."

A few more goodbyes, and then he was following Caitlyn out the front door. She seemed to be hurrying a little. Eager to get on with contacting Jake, he supposed.

She started down the few steps from the porch to the sidewalk. At the bottom she stopped abruptly, clinging to the railing, her face averted.

"Caitlyn, what is it?" Alarmed, he put his arm around her for support. "Are you ill?"

"No." She looked up at him. Tears spilled over onto her cheeks, but she was smiling. "We've done it, Steve. We've really done it."

His heart seemed to be caught in a vise. "Yes." It was all he could say. "We've done it."

Chapter Fifteen

Caitlyn hurried down the church hallway toward the grief center, on her way to pick up the twins from their session with Olga. Twenty-four busy hours had passed since their confrontation with General Willis. So much had been accomplished that it seemed impossible it had only been a day.

She'd been too busy to think about anything personal, and perhaps that was just as well. She hadn't quite assimilated the things she'd revealed about herself in that emotional exchange.

As for what Steve had revealed—no, she didn't want to consider what that meant for him. Or for them, if there was a *them*.

Olga came out of the children's center as Caitlyn reached it, her face breaking into a huge smile. "Caitlyn. I have been hoping to see you today so that I could say how happy I am at your accomplishment. It is an answer to our prayers."

"Not just my accomplishment," she said quickly. "Many people worked to make this happen. To tell you the truth, I'm still amazed that we succeeded."

She paused, considering the words. When had she become so pleased to share the credit for a success in which she'd participated?

Olga surveyed her. "The children are playing a game with the volunteers. Do you have time to wait until they have finished?"

She glanced at her watch. "Yes, of course."

"Come into my office, then." Olga opened the door. "We will have a little cup of tea."

She wasn't sure she wanted tea, but she let herself be led into Olga's small, cozy office, eclectic in its mixture of things Russian and Texan. Olga busied herself with an electric kettle, chattering away about the children's activities while she did.

The cozy room and Olga's voice were oddly soothing. Caitlyn leaned back in the rocking chair that was the visitor's chair. She hadn't slowed down in what felt like days.

Olga set a delicate china cup and saucer on the small table, and Caitlyn was reminded of Miss Willis. It looked like something she would use.

"You have been working hard for weeks on this project." Olga settled in the chair opposite her, balancing her own cup and saucer. "Now, when it is finished, will come the letdown."

"I guess that's true." Caitlyn took a sip of the pale brew, inhaling its mint fragrance. "The euphoria of succeeding has worn off." She'd often felt that way after a big case, so why should she be surprised at the feeling now?

"And with the end of your part in all this, Ali's future is in other people's hands," Olga said. "So you are at loose ends."

Caitlyn nodded. "I suppose that's true." She hadn't really paused to consider that.

"I understand, because it is the same for me. I work with a child or a family for weeks or months, and I become very attached to them. But then they move on. And I must be content that I did my best."

"I hadn't thought of it that way." She took another sip of the tea, feeling its relaxing warmth moving through her. "What we've accomplished for Ali and his grandfather is very satisfying."

Olga nodded. "It is. Still, I suppose you often experience that kind of satisfaction in your law practice, too."

Did she? She found herself looking at that question with a skeptical eye. Did she feel the personal involvement in her ordinary cases? The answer was no.

Well, that was natural enough. At the firm, she usually dealt with business issues, not with a little boy who needed a family. She might have an intellectual sense of triumph, but not an emotional one.

Was she really comparing the two? There was no comparison between a part-time job with a nonprofit and a career with a prestigious law firm.

Olga, bless her heart, had a way of leading you into thinking of things you really hadn't considered before, and maybe didn't want to consider now. Maybe a change of subject was a good idea.

"I've been meaning to mention to you that the twins haven't heard anything from Whitney and John in several days."

"They haven't?" Olga made a note on the pad at her elbow. "Their unit may simply be out on a mission or in an area where there is fighting, so that they don't have time to communicate. I'll see if I can find out anything." She raised an eyebrow as she looked at Caitlyn. "Things are a little better with you and the twins, yes?"

"Yes, I guess they are." She hesitated, but Olga should know what was happening with the twins in order to counsel them appropriately. "They had a rough time of it on their mother's birthday. We all did, as a matter of fact, but I think we crossed a bridge or two in getting through it together."

Olga nodded. "Sometimes it's in the most difficult times that the most progress is made. You're finding that, I think."

"I suppose I am." She looked down at the liquid in her cup. "I've finally had to admit that I've been angry at Carolyn."

"Naturally," Olga said placidly.

"It doesn't seem natural to me," she protested. "My sister is dead. I should be sad, but not angry."

"The anger is a part of grief for everyone. It takes different forms for different people, but it has to be dealt with."

She thought about what Steve had said about confronting her emotions where Carolyn was concerned. "I guess I need to come to terms with those feelings, but I don't know how."

"You're talking about it instead of hiding from it," Olga pointed out. "That's a good first step."

She had felt a sense of relief since she'd come out with her feelings in that painful interview with the general. She hadn't wanted to, certainly hadn't planned it, but when she saw her own emotions mirrored in the general's, she'd had to speak.

"What comes next?" She managed a smile. "I know it might not be that cut-and-dried, but for the twins' sake, I have to work on this."

"I understand. You're a lawyer, and you are used to identifying a problem and then working on a solution. This is not that complicated, although it can be hard to do. Forgiving. And being forgiven." Olga smiled, perhaps a little sadly. "We all need that at times."

Her throat tightened with a familiar ache. "Carolyn's not here to forgive. Or to forgive me."

Olga leaned forward, patting Caitlyn's hand. "Carolyn is in God's hands now, and God knows her heart. And yours. Talk to Him about it. Talk to her, even, as if she could hear you. Let God show you what is needed, my dear."

"That's it?" She looked at Olga, finding comfort in the warmth of her expression.

"Yes." Olga rose. "I will check on the children. Just sit and finish your tea."

She should get up. Go on to the next thing—take the children home, help Mama with supper. Instead she leaned back in the rocker.

Is that what I need, Father? Tears stung her eyes. *I want so much to be a good mother to those children. I wish I had been a better sister to Carolyn.*

Forgive, Olga had said. And be forgiven.

I forgive you, Carolyn. I forgive you for dying, for leaving us, for forcing me into a new life. Please forgive me. Forgive me for being judgmental, for thinking my choices were so much better than yours. Forgive me for not being a better sister.

All was still in the small room. Peace seemed to settle into Caitlyn's heart.

Thank You, Father.

The sound of the door opening made her turn around. Amanda and Josie rushed in, and she held out her arms to them, her love overflowing.

* * *

Steve sat at his desk, a half-written letter of condolence in front of him for the family of a casualty. He couldn't seem to concentrate, and he wouldn't let the writing of those letters become rote.

He put down his pen and folded his hands, staring at the paper in front of him as he tried to form a prayer. The problem was that he honestly didn't know how to pray in this situation.

He did know what he'd advise anyone else to do, didn't he? Pray anyway, and tell God exactly that. Maybe it was time to take his own advice.

Father, I'm coming to You in need of guidance. I have feelings for Caitlyn. I can't deny that any longer. But I can't—

What? What couldn't he do? He couldn't even articulate his emotions in his prayers. So he couldn't possibly hope to spell them out to Caitlyn.

She has her own grief to deal with now, Lord. I know that. I shouldn't do or say anything that would complicate things for her. Shouldn't I just try to be a friend? Isn't that enough right now for both of us?

He hesitated. Was he really asking for God's guidance? Or was he superimposing his own answers instead of listening for God's word?

He clenched his hands tighter together. *Please, Father...*

The telephone rang. He reached out, clearing his throat as he picked up the receiver. "Hello. Chaplain Steve here."

"Chaplain Steve, you have to come right away." A child's voice, and it took a moment to recognize it as Amanda's.

"Amanda, calm down. Does your grammy know you're on the phone? What's wrong?"

"It's Auntie Caitlyn."

His heart seemed to stop. "What is it? Is she hurt? Is anyone else there?" He fumbled for the cell phone in his pocket, trying to think what to do. Keep Amanda on the line, call 911—

"No." Amanda's words were interrupted by a sob. "She's not hurt. She wants to take us away."

"Take you away," he echoed, trying to make sense of the child's words. "Take you away where? What makes you think that?"

"Me and Josie heard her. She telled Grammy about a job in the city, and how we'd all have to go and live there." She choked a little. "Please come, Chaplain Steve. I don't want to go away."

"I'll be right there." He was standing even as he spoke. "Don't worry, sweetheart. Everything is going to be all right."

He hung up and hurried for the door. He had to get there. Had to talk some sense into Caitlyn before it was too late.

What on earth was she thinking of? She'd said she knew she had to put the children first. She'd said she loved them and wanted to be a good parent to them. How could she possibly even consider taking them away from everything they knew and loved?

The questions kept bouncing around in his mind as he drove off post and crossed the bridge that led to Prairie Springs. He fumed at every stoplight, wanting to hurry. Needing to hurry, to tell Caitlyn that she couldn't possibly do this to them. To him.

No. He backed away from that thought in a hurry. This was about what was best for the children.

The drive seemed to take twice as long as usual.

Everyone in Prairie Springs had apparently decided to be out and about just when he had to get there.

Finally he pulled up at the house. Maybe he should have called first to be sure Caitlyn was home. She could be at the office. He'd been so upset by Amanda's call that he hadn't even thought to ask her when this happened or where her aunt was now.

He crossed the lawn quickly to the porch, jogged up the steps and rang the bell, trying to form some coherent argument in his mind. But he couldn't. All he could think was that she couldn't possibly go.

Caitlyn opened the door. "Steve, hi. I wasn't expecting you."

"I know." He glanced past her to the hallway. Everything seemed quiet. "Are Betty and the children at home?"

She stepped back, gesturing for him to come in. "Mama took the girls to the park, since it's a little cooler today. If you want to see them, they should be back in about an hour."

"I've come to talk with you." He studied her face, trying to discern something different there, but she looked the same as always. Beautiful.

"Come on back to the family room." She walked ahead of him toward the rear of the hallway. "Is it something new about Ali? Do you have an arrival date yet?"

"Not yet." He hadn't even thought about Ali since Amanda's call. "They'll let me know as soon as there's space on a flight for him, but it could be fairly short notice."

"Well, everything's set as far as the medical team is concerned. And I understand from Miss Willis that the general has a crew working overtime to turn a guest bedroom into a perfect haven for a little boy."

They reached the family room. The rug was cluttered with a dollhouse and an array of tiny furniture. Caitlyn stepped over it and gestured toward the chintz-covered sofa.

"Have a seat. Sorry about the mess, but they'd just haul it all out again when they get back from the playground, so it was hardly worth clearing up." She smiled. "Besides, singing the 'time to clean up' song once a day is enough."

He stood where he was. "I don't need a seat. Just an answer. How can you possibly move the girls and Betty to New York just because of your job?"

She just stared at him. "What—how do you know about that?"

So it was true. Anger boiled up in him, mixed with pain. "How could you do that? Those children are already dealing with enough grief and heartache in their lives. How can you even consider taking them away from their home, their friends, everything they know and love, just so you can run back to your job?"

Caitlyn was staring at him with an expression he couldn't read. Finally she spoke. "Actually it wasn't the same job. I've been offered a junior partnership if I return to New York immediately to handle a case that's come up."

"And that's more important than the children?" He wanted to grab her, hang on to her, force her to understand. "You can't uproot them. You can't leave."

You can't leave me. That was what he wanted to say, but he couldn't.

"I don't understand you, Caitlyn. I thought I knew you. I thought you were proud of what you'd accomplished here, that you—"

"I turned it down."

He could only stare at her. "What?"

"I turned the offer down."

Caitlyn was quaking inside, but she kept her back straight and her head high. If she could face down an opposing attorney in a courtroom, she could handle confronting Steve.

Except that in a courtroom, her heart wouldn't be torn by the accusation in Steve's voice.

"But I thought..." He let that trail off, looking as if he'd just been hit by a two-by-four.

"It's pretty obvious what you thought." She struggled to control the pain and anger. *How could you think that of me, Steve? Don't you know me any better than that?* "How did you know anything about the offer to begin with?"

"Amanda called me."

"Amanda," she echoed. "But how did she know? Mama and I certainly didn't discuss it in front of the children."

"I guess she was listening."

"I guess she was." Anger made her words staccato. "So you took the word of an eavesdropping five-year-old and jumped to the conclusion that I was going to pack up the girls and my mother and jaunt off to New York with them."

"I didn't—"

"Yes. You did." Her hands clenched. "That's exactly what you did. I thought we were beginning to know each other. I guess I was wrong."

He shook his head. "Look, I'm sorry. I guess I overreacted. Amanda was so upset that all I could think of to do was get over here and try to stop you. If I'd thought it through, I'd have realized she might have misunderstood."

His obvious emotion seemed to take away some of her anger. It was satisfying to know that he cared enough to act without thinking when he thought she was going to leave.

He put out a hand, as if to placate her. "I apologize. As a friend, I shouldn't have jumped to conclusions about you."

As a friend.

She wanted to be his friend. Of course she did. But even as she thought it, she knew she wanted something more. And it was something she could never have unless Steve was able to open up to her.

"No. You shouldn't have." She took a deep breath, trying to sort out her words. "You know, as much as anyone, how much I've changed since I came back to Prairie Springs."

He nodded. He seemed to be relaxing a little, apparently convinced the crisis was over.

But she couldn't let it go at that.

"I know now what's important in my life. And it isn't just about doing the right thing for the twins and my mother. It's not just about sacrificing what I want for them."

She struggled her way through the maze of emotions, sensing that she had to articulate this as much for her own sake as his.

"I've found out that God has put me here for a purpose, and that here, with my mother and the children, is where my true happiness lies. I can't uproot them. I'll make a new life here."

"I'm glad for you." Steve's voice had become husky, and his eyes shone as if with unshed tears.

She focused on his face, praying for the courage to say what she felt had to be said. "I've opened my heart to you about why I'm staying. Now it's your turn. Why do you want me to stay?"

His expression became guarded. "Why, I…I told you. For the children, for Betty. I…I know you're going to be happier here…"

His stumbling over his answer told her everything she needed to know, even if it wasn't the answer she'd hoped for, and her heart seemed to turn to stone in her chest.

"It's all right, Steve." She longed to turn away and evade his gaze, but she wouldn't do that. She'd face this through.

"It's all right," she said again. "You don't need to say anything else. I understand. I know you can't say what you don't feel."

He stared at her for a long moment, and it seemed that he was trying to articulate some new argument. Then, quite suddenly, he shook his head. In a moment, he was gone.

Chapter Sixteen

By the time Steve's mind actually started registering, he realized he'd driven back onto the post, as if on automatic pilot. But not to his office or the chapel. Instead his heart had brought him to the Monument for the Fallen.

He didn't want to be here. Hadn't been here, in fact, since Elaine's death.

But something stronger than his own desires seemed to be pushing him. He parked at the curb, got out, and walked slowly across the grass toward the monument.

The designer had created a parklike space with grass and trees surrounding the central monument. Benches faced the center, and around the perimeter stood marble columns bearing the names of the fallen who had passed through Fort Bonnell.

He sat down on the closest bench, trying not to look at the columns. He didn't want to wonder which of them carried Elaine's name.

Why do you want me to stay?

Caitlyn's question had been simple enough. It was the answer that was difficult.

Or maybe it hadn't been simple at all, because of what he knew lay beneath it. They both understood that she was really asking whether there was a possibility of a future for them.

It had taken courage for Caitlyn to bare her soul to him, telling him what lay in her heart. Once she'd have said that relying on someone else for her happiness was the one thing she couldn't do. Now she was willing to risk heartbreak to let him know how she felt.

He cared about her. So why couldn't he say that?

Maybe he just didn't have enough courage. Or maybe he had some unfinished business to take care of first.

I can't.

That was the coward's answer, wasn't it? In the years he'd been here, he'd tried to comfort other people in their grief. Maybe he'd even succeeded, with God's help.

But he hadn't ever faced his own.

I can't.

Struggling to focus on anything else, he watched as a small group of people crossed the strip of green. A middle-aged man and woman, holding hands as if for support. A younger woman, pushing a toddler in a stroller, her head held defiantly high.

They paused at the center monument for a moment, reading its inscription. He didn't have to go closer to know what it said.

Dedicated to our fallen comrades. We will never forget.

The younger woman bent, taking something from the

basket of the stroller. It was a single red rose. She laid it reverently on the plinth of the monument.

The group stood for a moment longer, heads bowed.

He shouldn't watch them. He should get up, go to them, try to offer solace. That was his role in life. But he couldn't.

They crossed the grass again, obviously knowing which column to approach. There they stopped. The older woman's shoulders shook with sobs, and the man put his arm around her. For a moment none of them moved.

Then the young woman bent to lift the child from the stroller. She took the child's small hand, using it to trace the letters on the column. A name. Just a name, but it was all the world to them.

Steve buried his face in his hands. *I can't.* But he couldn't stop it, not now. The images flooded back. The sights, the sounds, the smells.

Chaos. It had been chaos when the roadside bomb went off.

He'd started to run, shaking off the soldier who tried to pull him to shelter, knowing that the blast had been close to Elaine's vehicle. Too close.

She had been gone when he reached her. He hadn't been able to offer the simplest of comfort to her in her dying moments. All he could do was hold her and weep for what might have been.

It should have been me.

The words shocked him. He knew all about survivor guilt. He'd dealt with it often enough. He'd thought he knew it so well that he couldn't possibly feel it himself, and yet there it was.

Father. His heart reached out in prayer before he formed

the conscious thought. *I feel guilty because I am alive and Elaine is gone. How can I forgive myself for that?*

The moment he asked the question he knew how it sounded. He knew what he would say to anyone else in that situation.

You are still here because God has plans for your life. That was what he would say, and it was as true for him as for anyone else he might counsel.

God had plans for his life, and surely those plans didn't involve shutting his heart away from the pain of loving. If they did, God wouldn't have brought Caitlyn into his life, challenging him to feel again.

He tilted his head back, eyes closed, feeling the tears on his cheeks.

He felt a touch on his hand and opened his eyes. It was the young mother, her expression hesitant. She glanced at the older couple, as if for encouragement, and they nodded, their faces tearstained.

"Do you have someone here, too?"

He nodded, understanding what she meant.

"We thought you might want this. To leave." She held out another rose. "Take it. We brought plenty."

His throat was tight. Now it was his turn to be ministered to. He couldn't speak, but he had to.

"Thank you." His voice choked. "I'd like that."

He stood, taking the flower. He should say something more to them, but they obviously didn't expect that. They walked away together, moving more freely now, as if they'd left some of their burden behind.

For a moment he didn't move. Then, holding the rose, he went to find Elaine's name.

* * *

Caitlyn forked Mama's oven-baked chicken tenders onto Amanda's plate and smiled at her. "Okay now?"

Amanda grinned. "I'm okay. We get to stay here in Grammy's house forever and ever."

"And Grammy and Auntie Caitlyn will take care of us," Josie added.

Mama set a casserole of scalloped potatoes on the table and bent over to hug each of them. "And no more listening in on grown-up people's conversations. Misunderstandings can only lead to trouble."

Amanda's face clouded. "Chaplain Steve's not mad at us, is he?"

"No, I'm sure he's not." Caitlyn managed to keep a smile on her face, regardless of the pain in her heart caused by just hearing his name. She sat down. "Whose turn is it to ask the blessing?"

"Mine," Josie said. She folded her hands and squinted up her eyes. "God is great, God is good, and we thank Him for our food. By His hands we all are fed, give us, Lord, our daily bread. Amen."

"Amen," Caitlyn echoed. *And let me be content with what You give me, Father, even though Steve is not part of my future. Amen.*

It was going to hurt for a while. There was no doubt about that. But she'd be all right. They'd all be all right.

The doorbell rang.

"I declare, if it's not the telephone, it's the doorbell interrupting dinner." Her mother started to rise, but Caitlyn got up quickly.

"I'll get it, Mama. You sit still."

Before she reached the door, she could see Steve's tall figure through the glass panels. Her heart began to pound.

She opened the door. His face was drawn, and she couldn't read his expression.

"Can we talk? Please?"

She nodded. "My mother and the twins are in the kitchen—" And they'll hear everything we have to say to each other. But he surely realized that.

Steve glanced around, as if looking for inspiration. Behind her, she could hear Josie asking who was there, while Amanda clamored to be excused from the table to find out. On the lawn next door, a clutch of teenage boys were playing a noisy game of touch football.

"Come on." He grabbed her hand. "We can sit in the truck. At least it'll be cool."

She wanted to protest, but he tugged her through the door. Giving in, she let herself be led to the pickup. She climbed into the passenger seat.

Steve hurried around the vehicle, got in and started the engine. A welcome blast of cool air came from the air-conditioning vents.

"I guess I didn't plan this very well for a serious talk," he said.

Her heart began to thud again. "Is that what this is?"

He nodded. "I'm sorry. About before."

"It doesn't matter." She didn't want to rehash it, because if they did, she was bound to end up in tears. "If that's all—" She reached for the door handle.

He caught her hand before she could open the door. "No, that's not all."

He was very close in the narrow quarters of the front

seat. She could see the fine lines around his eyes, the curve of his ear, the faint stubble on his chin that said he hadn't shaved since this morning. Her breath was doing something very strange, and she had to force herself to inhale.

He leaned back a little, looking at her. "Do you know where I went when I left here earlier?"

She shook her head.

"I went to the Monument for the Fallen." His jaw tightened. "Elaine's name is on it. I'd never even gone to see it before."

She really couldn't breathe, which seemed odd to think about at a time like this. "Why did you go now?"

He was silent for a moment. "I think God sent me there because I needed to say goodbye. And I needed to say goodbye because He brought you into my life."

"I don't want you to forget her."

"I know." His fingers closed over hers. "I know that. But there's a difference between not forgetting someone and using that person's death as a reason not to let anyone else in."

"Steve—" She said his name, troubled.

He took a breath, closing his eyes for a second. "I realized today that I've been feeling guilty for being alive when she was gone. I couldn't face it, but that feeling isn't right. That's not what she'd want for me, and it's certainly not what God wants for me."

Tears filled her eyes, and she tried to blink them back. "Are you all right now?"

He nodded. "Caitlyn, I want—"

"Wait." She put her fingers over his lips. "Let me say something first." She struggled to organize her thoughts. "The twins have to be my first concern now. I'm a mother.

If I get involved with anyone, it has to be serious, for their sake. And I can't rush to change anything—"

He kissed her fingers, derailing her train of thought entirely. "Can I say something now?"

She nodded.

"When I walked away from the monument today, I knew I was free to love. We can take as much time as you and the twins need, but know this. I'm ready to be serious—I want to love you and those girls forever."

There weren't any words to respond to that. Caitlyn drew his face toward hers and kissed him—a kiss filled with the promise of a new tomorrow for all of them, with God's help.

Epilogue

With Steve holding her hand, Caitlyn hurried into the kitchen at Children of the Day, eager to share the good news he'd brought. Anna, Olga and Sarah sat at the table, coffee cups in front of them. Anna looked up instantly at their entrance, her eyes questioning.

"We have an announcement to make." Caitlyn glanced at Steve. "You tell them."

He grinned at her and then turned to the others. "I just got the word. The flight is all set up. Ali will be arriving in Texas next week."

"That's wonderful!" Anna grabbed first Caitlyn and then Steve in a huge hug. "I can't wait to greet that little boy. Does he have a medical attendant for the long flight here?"

"A nurse is coming with him. And David Ryland, a chopper pilot who's been seeing a lot of him and who is being rotated home, has arranged to come on the same plane. So he'll have plenty of company."

"You did a good job. Both of you," Olga said. Something in her bright eyes suggested that she knew what they weren't telling yet.

Caitlyn glanced at Steve, suspecting that her love was shining in every look, every touch, giving her away.

"Not just us. So many people have worked to make this happen. I have a feeling that the general pulled strings that went all the way to the Pentagon."

"One little life, saved from destruction," Anna said, and for a moment her expression was touched by sorrow, and Caitlyn knew that she was thinking of those who were lost.

"One at a time," she said softly, taking Anna's hand. "God's leading us to save one at a time."

Anna nodded, her face brightening. "We do His work in the world."

"Amen," Steve said, and each of them echoed the word.

* * * * *

In August 2008, don't miss the second
Homecoming Heroes book,
LONE STAR SECRET *by Lenora Worth.*

Dear Reader,

Thank you for picking up this first installment of the brand-new HOMECOMING HEROES series. All of the authors hope you enjoy our stories as much as we've enjoyed working together to write this series for you.

I was especially moved to be writing a book that featured a man whose counterparts in real life, the military chaplains, are true heroes. Chaplains have been part of our military forces since the revolution, and they serve selflessly in very difficult situations, bringing comfort, hope and the assurance of God's love to our men and women in uniform.

I hope you'll let me know how you felt about this story, and I'd love to send you a signed bookmark or my brochure of Pennsylvania Dutch recipes. You can write to me at Steeple Hill Books, 233 Broadway, Suite 1001, New York, NY 10279, e-mail me at marta@martaperry.com or visit me on the Web at www.martaperry.com.

Blessings,

Marta Perry

QUESTIONS FOR DISCUSSION

1. Can you understand the conflict Caitlyn faced when she felt she had to give up the life she wanted in order to care for her sister's children? Have you ever struggled to balance two seemingly conflicting needs? How did you manage?

2. Steve follows in his father's footsteps as a military chaplain, inspired by the example he set. Do you know anyone who's made that kind of life choice? What difficulties are involved in following in a parent's profession?

3. Caitlyn finds that coming home again is a chance to build a stronger relationship with her mother. How have you found that dealing with troubles can sometimes bring a family closer together?

4. Caitlyn's growing dedication to the twins gave her the courage to do things she'd never expected to. What do you think drove her, even when she was afraid?

5. Steve ministered to others in their grief, when the truth was that he hadn't dealt with his own. What experiences have you had of God's help in time of grief? Is there anything that you tend to hold back from God? What is it?

6. The scripture verse for this story is a very short one,

but it packs some powerful meaning in a few words. Have you found this verse to be true in your life? How?

7. Caitlyn finds a community and acceptance in the friends she makes when she returns to Prairie Springs. Have you had the experience of feeling like a fish out of water in a new place? Who made you feel welcome?

8. Both Caitlyn and Steve are challenged to be honest about their grief. Do you think we turn to God more readily when times are difficult? Why or why not?

9. The scripture passage tells us to bear one another's burdens in order to fulfill the law of Christ. In what ways do you try to bear someone else's burdens?

10. Do you think this passage applies only to the physical help we give one another? In what other ways can we provide support to our brothers and sisters in Christ?

11. Has God ever called you to bear the burden of someone you disliked or disapproved of? How did you cope with that?

12. When you have an opportunity to welcome someone new to your church or community, how do you do that?

13. Which character in the story did you feel was living the most Christlike life? Why?

14. Is it most difficult to be honest with yourself about

your fears and shortcomings, or to be honest with someone else? Why?

15. Does the story give you the sense that the twins will overcome the loss of their parents? How do you think it will affect their lives?

Love Inspired.
HISTORICAL

INSPIRATIONAL HISTORICAL ROMANCE

After an unhappy marriage, Charity Beal avoids men. But she can't keep her distance from Thorne Blackwell, a rugged shipping magnate who needs her help on a grueling journey through Oregon to look for his brother. Charity's kindness and faith awakens Thorne to a new strength—but before they explore a relationship, Thorne must protect them both from the danger that follows them.

Look for

Wilderness Courtship

by

VALERIE HANSEN

Available August 2008
wherever books are sold.

www.SteepleHill.com

Steeple Hill®

LIH82793

TITLES AVAILABLE NEXT MONTH

Don't miss these four stories in August

HER PERFECT MAN by Jillian Hart
The McKaslin Clan
New neighbor Chad Lawson seems too perfect. At least to Rebecca McKaslin, who's been burned by Prince Charming before. Yet, as Rebecca gets to know Chad, his reliable, friendly nature challenges her resistance to relationships. Maybe God put him in her life for a reason.

LONE STAR SECRET by Lenora Worth
Homecoming Heroes
David Ryland is about to fly his final military mission. Then he must face up to his past. His family was a mystery until his father confessed his parentage in a deathbed letter. A letter that Anna Terenkov knows *all* about. If David can open his heart to the truth, will he find room for Anna?

HIDDEN TREASURES by Kathryn Springer
All work and no play is Cade Halloway's motto. His new project: selling his family's vacation home. Yet Cade must wait until after his sister's wedding. And deal with photographer Meghan McBride. But what Cade doesn't know is that love is just one of many surprises to be discovered on the property!

BLUEGRASS HERO by Allie Pleiter
Kentucky Corners
Dust-covered cowboys are the norm at Gil Sorrent's ranch. Until a visit to Emily Montague's bath shop has them cleaning up their acts. Now they spend more time courting than working. Gil is determined to give Emily a piece of his mind, but it's his heart she's after.